Break Away

Cuffed: Book Three
An Erotica

By: Carissa McIntyre

Wow, this is my fifth erotica book everyone, and what a rush this has been!

Thank you to every single person who has come along for the ride over the last year and a half.

Homeless, to self-published, my entire life has changed, and I owe so much love and thanks and gratitude to all of you for your amazing support, encouragement and the occasional kick in the ass to keep me going!

Because what are books without readers who love them?

Enjoy this novel my friends! Keep on reading, and soaking up the finer things in life. You know what I'm talking about...

Much Love,
Lady Mack, xoxo

This book is a work of fiction. Any references to historical events, real people, or real locales are used factiously. Any names, characters, places, and incidents are the product of the author's imagination, and any resemblance to actual events, or locales, or persons, living or dead, is entirely coincidental.

Break Away
Copyright December 2018 Carissa McIntyre
Published by Lady Mack Publishing
All Rights Reserved, including the right of reproduction in whole or in part in any form.
Wrote in Canada.
Manufactured in the USA.
All Rights Reserved

Carissa McIntyre is a self-published author from Ontario Canada. Her work can be found at www.ladymackpublishing.com
Publishing / all other inquiries may be sent to: carissa.mcintyre@hotmail.ca

New Adult – Romance -Erotica

Carissa McIntyre
Copyright February 2017 by Carissa McIntyre
All Rights Reserved

ISBN: 9781790490073

Break Away
Book: Three

Chapter One

Occasional passing headlights traveling down the highway shine through the thick layer of bushes that Adam and Demi's car is tucked behind. The lights break through the darkness and cause a flickering white glow to appear on the hood in front of Demi. The shadows of branches and leaves dance back and forth across her pale arms and the front of the car, the light bringing everything in and out of focus for her in the dark of the late summer evening.

When there is enough light to make things out, she can see her bare arms sprawled out in front of her, her fingers spread wide open, helping support her weight and holding herself steady while she bends over the hood of the car, using it as leverage to thrust herself backwards. The car is still hot on her skin from all of the traveling they have done today, miles and miles underneath their tires, and the hood burns a little against her cool skin, but not enough for her to want to stop. The contrast is rather nice, causing her to shiver a little, and goosebumps to break out along the back of her legs.

Adam is standing right there behind her in the dark, taking her, pounding his hard cock into her, spreading her wide open, having his way with her, while they are hidden there on the side of the road. She can feel his hands gripping her hard around her naked waist, pulling her tightly into him, his skin warm on hers. She can hear the sound of his shoes slipping on the dirt under his feet as he thrusts his body into her over and over. His fingertips are holding so tightly onto her hips, digging into her, gripping her hip bones, bringing her into him time and time again, that she will certainly have small fingertip bruise marks there tomorrow as he takes her for all that he's worth, owning her, fucking her tight little hole.

The smell of the hot engine in front of her, with a light smell of oil and gas, and the dirt and wet damp leaves and road around them mix together and hit her nose, overwhelming her senses, her body so heightened already by the incredible way that she is feeling. She can see drops of water roll down the leaves to the left of the car, and the wet rain drops in the bushes glisten in the constant flashing of the headlights as they pass by only a few yards away from where they are hidden. The ground beneath her is rumbling slightly from all of the passing traffic traveling nearby. It's like she can smell, see and hear everything around them, all of her senses on overdrive.

And on top of all those sensations is the way her body is feeling right now, reacting to him, everything about her heated up like it's on fire, shaking and shuddering right down to her toes as Adam fucks her from behind. His hard cock is covered in her juices as it slides in and out of her tight hole, bottoming out in her, bringing them both closer and closer to an orgasm they are desperately craving and needing so badly, her pussy walls squeezing him ever so tightly.

The pair had pulled off the highway a half hour before this little rendezvous, having gotten themselves so worked up talking dirty to each other while Adam had been driving, getting carried away with each other while passing the time. So, feeling frisky, he had turned off the highway at the next exit and taken the first couple of turns he could find, which didn't take them very far from the highway in itself, but took them far enough away to be secluded behind this chunk of bushes.

They seemed to be on what looked like a highway service road, not likely to be used this late at night, giving them all the privacy they needed for this fun little road side quickie. But it also gave them both a naughty thrill though, to be so close to the highway and people passing them by, where they could possibly be seen and caught at any moment, despite the private feel. It gave them a sense of excitement, and danger, only adding to the taboo lifestyle they'd been living this entire time.

Once Adam had parked the car and stopped the engine, the world around them had calmed and quieted, and they took off their seat belts and were finally free to do whatever they wanted. Feeling so incredibly horny already, they took well advantage of that. They were all over each other in the front seat, grabbing at one another and making out heavily for a little while like they were teenagers at the make-out spot, still unable to get enough of one another, horny as all hell.

Even with all of the time they've been together since they first started dating after the kidnapping, weeks and weeks on end spent in constant close quarters, always driving and sharing hotel rooms, practically living together without either of them actually having a place to live and settle down in, they can still not get enough of one another. Their sexual drives are at an all-time high, and completely unsatisfiable. There is this burning passion and need to share everything together, to explore and learn about one another, to know every little thing about each other's bodies and how they work and what they want, what makes them each tick, scream, moan and beg for more. They crave one another sexually so badly that they're still fucking like horny rabbits every chance they get, even out in the open on the side of the road. There was practically nothing that would keep them from having one another, anywhere that they wanted or desired.

It has been over a week since they had left the hotel after the heist and had hit the road, with their bags packed once more, and a ton of money at their disposal, just wanting to put the miles between them and everything that had happened and leave everything behind them in the past where it belonged. But they had no real destination in mind now though, and no real purpose for their life at the moment anymore, both just desperately needing to get away from what had transpired.

Demi had mentioned wanting to go to the coast a few weeks before the heist had even happened, wanting to take some time off of everything that they'd been doing, all the driving, crime, and wild life they were living, and that was something that had stuck with Adam, and he'd brought it up once they'd gotten on the road. So that's where they were headed now, thinking that they could both use a little bit of time to just relax and enjoy their new life together, to get settled in with nothing on their minds but beach, booze and sex. Lots and lots of sex.

It may have been Demi's idea to start with, but Adam did agree with her wholeheartedly. It has been weeks and weeks of nonstop driving and chaos since the kidnapping, always on the go, living on the run, not really having the time to enjoy a real life, or at least, not really making the time. They lived solely off of take out foods and quick road side showers and were keeping the strangest hours, and none of those things were good for long periods of time. He had to admit, all of that was definitely taking a toll on them both.

And the idea seemed so important to Demi, that they take some time to rest, to recharge and to be together without constantly driving or living a life of crime, and so Adam made it important to him too. He would have done anything for her, been anywhere with her, under any circumstances that she needed or asked from him. A little time on the beach definitely didn't seem like that hard of a thing to do for her, with a comfy bed to sleep in every night, no early mornings, good food to eat and lots of sex. How could he complain?

They had taken turns driving towards the coast, laying low and not rushing the trip, sleeping the nights away in cheap motels on the side of the road and just taking in the sights that they saw along the way, knowing that they were going to reach their destination soon, and take a real break then. But all this constant time spent on the road was starting to make them both antsy, even before they reached the coast, and to cure the itch this time, they had started getting flirty and dirty to pass the time while driving, talking about fantasies and sexual ideas not yet explored between them yet, and then they decided to make a road side stop in the dark, still an hour out from the next city where they had planned to stop for the night. They just couldn't resist a quickie, between passion, need, horniness, and antsy boredom.

Their make out session in the car had escalated fast with the heat and excitement between them already so intense, and since they were stopped far enough away from the highway behind some bushes on a one lane dirt service road that no one seemed to use, and they likely wouldn't be seen, or caught, it wasn't long before they tumbled out of the car altogether, looking for more room to stretch their legs a little bit and have some more fun in this private little location they had found.

As soon as they had stepped out and shut the door behind them, Adam had grabbed her and pushed her up against the car, her ass pressed against the side of the hood, with one of his hands wrapped around her waist and the other wrapped around her throat lightly, pulling her face into his so that he could kiss her deeply, needing to taste her once more. Loving the soft feel of her lips and tongue.

Demi had opened her lips to him eagerly, accepting his probing tongue and letting him take her mouth, exploring her, his tongue awakening a tingling between her legs, thinking about how good it felt licking her there as well. At the same time that she kissed him back, she started pressing her body up against his, almost humping his leg, wrapping her arms around him and pulling him into her, wanting all of him, wanting him to know just how badly she needed him, just how horny she was to feel him inside of her.

He had let out a moan at her eagerness, loving how turned on she already was, how horny she always got for him, knowing that when he reached underneath her panties, he was going to find her dripping with wetness for him. Then he took a step back slightly, breaking their kiss. He looked her up and down a couple of times, taking her all in and giving her that smile that she loved to see as she watched him, thinking about what he wanted to do to her exactly.

Then he started stripping her, right there in the chilly night air, exposing her body and leaving her stark naked for his viewing pleasure, and any accidently passerby's to see. When he was done, he demanded that she turn around and bend over the hood of the car, and present herself to him. The authority in his voice always gave her chills, more powerful than the chills from the cold of the night, and those chills from him pulsed right though to her pussy, tingling like crazy, turning her on even more.

So now here they were, on the side of the road, outside in the night, giving their restless legs a chance to work themselves out while they were pressed up against the side of the front of the car. Adam had undone his belt and dropped his pants and boxers to his feet, and now the front of his bare thighs, sticky with sweat and a little bit of her juices, were rubbing against the back of Demi's tender goose bump covered legs, spread out wide in front of him, giving him access to all of her. She was moaning and groaning, throwing herself backwards against him, using the car as leverage to push herself into him harder and harder, matching his thrusts to fill her, wanting it all.

Adam was so worked up from of all their kissing and teasing foreplay they had gotten up to in the car earlier that he knew it wasn't going to be long before he blew his load into her. But he also knew that between the speed that he was pounding into her sweet pussy, slamming into her as he took her harder and harder, and by the moans that she was making, that she was going to be cumming soon too. The feeling of his cock sliding in and out of her wet hole was amazing as she squeezed him tighter and tighter, turning them both on like crazy.

Then she started moaning louder, throwing her hips back into him and wiggling her ass wildly, really getting into it more and more. "Oh, yes, baby, take me, fuck me," she said with her face turned back slightly over her shoulder towards him, looking at him in the eyes, "Does this make you feel good? Do I turn you on? Do you like fucking my tight pussy?" Adam let out a deep groan at her naughty talk, and thrust his dick into her even harder, feeling her vagina almost swallow him as his balls tightened and slapped the back of her legs. "Yes, baby," he moaned back, "I love your slippery hole, so wet, tight, milking my cock. I want to feel your walls tighten around me while you cum all over my big dick, cum with me baby." She loved hearing him dirty talk right back to her as they both grew more and more comfortable with each other, able to tell one another exactly what they wanted sexually, and she felt her stomach clench in excitement and her pussy tightened as she felt herself grow closer to orgasm too.

Adam reached up with one free hand and grabbed at one of her breasts, cupping it and squeezing it, pinching and pulling on her nipple a few times, before moving over to the other one, making them both perky and hard as his hands moved back and forth to caress them both, teasing her. Then he slid his hand down her soft smooth stomach, his middle finger making its way between her silky folds, spreading her lips open to expose her and finding her hard little clit, buried under its hood. She moaned and threw herself into him as he rubbed her nub a few times, teasing her even more, before removing his hand and taking hold of her body once more and really starting to thrust his cock in and out of her.

Now they were both slamming into each other, picking up speed, and Adam's fingers were already leaving marks as he gripped her tighter and tighter, pinning her into him as he fucked her hard. His thumbs pressed into her ass cheeks, spreading her open for him, exposing her little ass as well, and he watched it pucker and wink at him as he fucked her. His cock was filling her roughly, bottoming out in her, hitting her cervix and rubbing her g spot as he filled her deeply, and then he started to twitch inside of her.

This was too much for him, and finally pushed him over the edge. He let out a loud yell, no longer even caring if anyone heard them out here in the night. His balls tightened and he reached up and grabbed her by her shoulder, pulling her in even closer to him, pressing her back into his sweaty chest as her vagina started to tighten and clench around him, and she let out a cry of her own.

Demi started to shudder and shake as she came hard, feeling her body let go and her orgasm over take her, everything tightening and spasming, causing her to almost see stars and feel faint, like she was falling, leaning her body back into him for support. She felt his cock spasm inside of her and hot cum began to fill her, mixing with her own juices, the wetness coating her pussy lips and dripping down between her thighs and out onto him, soaking them. Both of their bodies were sticky and sweaty as they slowly stopped moving and just rested into each other, leaning up against the side of the hood.

    Then Adam spun her around and held her close as they lay up against the car, both of them breathing heavy, his arms wrapped around her in the dark, holding her, kissing her softly and gently along the back of her neck and her shoulders. "I love you," he whispered to her, and he smiled as he heard her say it back, relaxing his body into hers and touching her lightly, giving them both a minute to come down from their sexual high and catch their breath before they cleaned themselves up and hit the road again.

Chapter Two

It's just under an hour later since they'd finished up from their rendezvous and now they are back in the car, driving down the highway once more, headlights passing them by in the dark. The mood between them is a lot more relaxed now that they've shared a few orgasms together, and time passes a lot faster while they drive this time. Traffic has been backed up though, and they are finally getting close to the hotel where they've planned to pull over for the night and catch up on some rest, the hotel that they just couldn't make it to in time before they had to pull over for some road side fun earlier.

They are now only about a day or so drive from the actual beach line coast in Los Angeles where they plan to stay for a while and take a load off. They could probably do the drive in less than a day if they really hit the pavement hard and took turns driving straight through, burning up the miles, but they're both feeling far too drained for that, and tonight they plan to book the hotel for two nights instead of one, to catch up on some much needed sleep, real sleep without an alarm clock. Sleep without having to get up at the crack of dawn and hit the road before traffic gets too busy. Real sleep like the dead sleep. Relaxing in the morning with nowhere to be, at least for one day. It will be the first real long rest that they've had since they left the hotel after the heist and hit the road again, and it is very much needed with both of them still on edge after everything that happened.

Despite all of this time that they've spent cramped up together in the car, in such close quarters, constantly traveling and sharing stories and enjoying their new life together, they still haven't sat down and truly had a real long chat about what happened with the robbery. They haven't actually discussed in detail about what Demi had done, and her involvement with the wife, and about how that made either of them feel, or if it had any real effect on their relationship at all.

Sure, they had shared a quick chat the day after in the hotel room, about how hot it had been for Adam to watch what had transpired between the girls, and about some of the kinky scenes that he hadn't gotten a chance to peek in on, but nothing that had transpired that night other than the actual sexual aspect had fully been talked about out in the open; how each of them really felt about it, and how things were between them now.

Neither of them had really wanted to bring it up while they were driving in the car either, considering they were sort of trapped together with nowhere to go if the conversation went south, so it was a topic that they had both swallowed and put off, avoiding carefully in conversation, keeping their thoughts to themselves. Over time though, that was starting to grate on them both, and making them each uneasy with how the other may be feeling, all that uncertainty and all the questions building up. All of the what if's and the unknowns. That, plus all of the driving they have done, nonstop for what seems like months now, is taking more of a toll of them than they realized at first. They're achy, and miserable more often than not, and they both seem to be constantly anxious.

While they have been back in the car and driving once more this evening, Adam finds himself thinking about the engagement ring in his pocket that he occasionally reaches down to play with between his fingertips, flipping it over and over in there, feeling the rock dig into his skin through the material of his pants. He is constantly thinking about the ring, he can't seem to stop, and the how of it, how he's actually going to ask her to marry him, running all the possible scenarios through his head again and again is also consuming him. It's starting to consume him and interrupt the good feelings that he's been having while driving around with her.

And that seems ridiculous to him, because this should make him happier than anything, wanting to propose to her, and spend the rest of his life with her. This should be a magical thing. He just doesn't know when the right time is going to be to give it to her, and he can't decide what she would want from him. And that uncertainty is eating away at him, making him doubt his ideas and himself.

Is she going to want him to plan something fun, or romantic, like some fancy scavenger hunt, or a lovely dinner or walk somewhere with gorgeous scenery around them for the perfect story to tell later on? Or should he just wait until the right moment presents itself, no matter what that might be, and simply wing it and be spontaneous about the whole thing?

And because of all this unspoken baggage and tension, the uncertainty and history between them now, shit they keep putting off that's continuing to build, he can't truly tell in his heart what she is going to say, or how she is going to react. Marriage isn't something that they've talked about much, and they don't have the most normal of relationships right now either. This whole thing between them was far more than a rush of money, crime and an undeniable sexual high. They were building a life around this, and it was time to maybe stop and think about things more clearly, and talk honestly between them about what they wanted to do with their future together.

All Adam does know for sure certainty though, the only thing that is crystal clear in his thoughts and feels right deep down in his soul is that he has to give her this ring, he has to propose to her and make this happen. And he has to do it while they are here on vacation. He wants to be her man, and he needs her to be his wife. He needs to know he's going to spend his entire life with her. He needs to make her his. He doesn't even know where this dire need has come from, but it's there, and he can't deny it. He loves her so much, he doesn't even care if it's too soon, or not well thought out, or if it's out of character for either of them, or even if it isn't normal at all.

There are some disadvantages to starting off your relationship as one of your girlfriends kidnappers, snatching her out of her bed in the middle of the night and holding her hostage for ransom, Adam finds himself thinking a bit bitterly, and one of those disadvantages is that your relationship is going to start off anything but normal. Especially if your girlfriend is someone like Demi, and already had huge insecurities and trust issues before she was ever even kidnapped. Now, she can't seem to shut her mind off to the unlimited amount of doubts that seem to fill it.

Adam finds himself thinking once more, that he wishes he could have met her under any other circumstances. Maybe through friends, set up on a blind date or at random, or maybe while out at the bar one night, or hell, maybe even at the grocery store. He doesn't care. He just wishes it hadn't have been because of that ridiculous plan of Brandon's, to kidnap a widow's daughter and make a quick huge sum of money. He wouldn't change it, knowing now that's how he would met her, but he still thinks about the whole thing with resentment and a touch of regret.

There are now some major trust issues and boundaries to work on, which he realizes are not going to be things that are going to go away any time soon, as much as he would love for all of this to just go away overnight. This is something they may always have to work on, if they really want this relationship to work for the rest of their lives.

There are also many things that don't happen naturally this way, living on the run together like this, things that would have happened in a regular relationship as it progressed, if they had lived in their own homes to start with, and had gone about their own, normal lives. Like the first few overnights, getting to leave that first tooth brush at someone's place, developing a genuine sense of trust, love, and hope for the future like regular, normal couples would. But then again, what is normal, he thinks. Nothing in his life was normal before this, that's the whole reason he had gotten involved in that ridiculous kidnapping in the first place, and normalcy certainly hadn't been a regular thing in her life either. So maybe they were both just winging it, trying to figure out what works for them, living their life in a way that felt good, as abnormal as it may be. Was that really such a bad thing?

Adam pulls himself out of his thoughts as he realizes he's already drove them to the hotel, and he's now stopped in front of the lobby, almost on auto pilot without even remembering driving through the traffic jam or even arriving in this city. Demi is talking to him about something, and it takes him another moment to tune himself back in and shake himself out of the mental hole that he'd fallen into. He really needs some rest.

He parks the car and they get out slowly, taking a moment to stretch their aching legs once more. Then they get checked in and settled into their room, both of them totally exhausted from all of their time on the road, and the late evening hour as it had fallen upon them quickly. Their little stop on the side of the road certainly hadn't helped their exhaustion either.

They barely say a word to each other as they bring their bags into the room, literally just tossing them against the wall and leaving them there for the morning. It wasn't long before they were both crashed on the hotel bed, laying side by side, still fully dressed, asleep before they'd hardly hit the pillow and whispered goodnight, and I love you.

Chapter Three

 The sound of the waves crashing against the beach, falling back with the tide before crashing forwards again is so soothing, it's like music to her ears, mingling in with the occasional cry of a sea bird. The sand is hot between her toes, and she gives them a wiggle, allowing the sand to slide through. The sun is high in the sky, shining so brightly into her eyes that she has to squint, she can barely see, especially as it reflects off the water to the left of her. But from what she can make out, all around her is simply beautiful sandy beach, ocean, and a fluffy cloudy blue sky, as far as she can see in every direction. It is an absolutely breathtaking view, and there doesn't seem to be another person in sight to share it with.
 The wind is blowing her hair back out of her face, whipping it out in long strands behind her, bringing the scent of the salty ocean to her nose, and she has this total feeling of happiness and carefree release, causing her face to break out into the biggest smile that she's made in a long time.
 All of these emotions that are surrounding her are feelings she's felt so seldom in her life, especially lately, with all of the chaos that she's found herself living in as her relationship with Adam progresses. She takes a moment to savor these feelings, finding herself wishing that she felt them more often.
 She has a look around her, twirling in circles, her bare toes digging into the sand for balance. She doesn't see Adam anywhere, but she can feel his presence there, she can almost smell him, and that's when she realizes that she must be dreaming. There are no buildings or people that she can see, no other sounds other than waves flowing and the odd cry of a sea bird in the distance, and she seems to be totally alone here in this perfect beach paradise. So she gives in to her dream and enjoys the sensations that she's experiencing, even the odd tingling feeling that she's starting to feel but can't explain, that seems to be starting

from deep down within her body.

So she keeps walking, breathing in the salty ocean smell, taking air deep into her lungs and smiling gently, letting herself soak in every feeling of her dream, even though she's slowly finding herself focusing more and more on the other feelings happening inside of her body, feelings of excitement, of joy, and of what almost feels like sexual pleasure as well, feelings that are slowly bringing her back into consciousness. Feelings, she's finding herself wondering, that don't seem to belong to this dream at all.

She's realizing that the dream around her is getting fuzzy, hard to focus on, and she can no longer see or concentrate on anything other than the sensations that she's feeling in her body, and she can't fight them any longer. She closes her eyes on her dream beach, and against the lingering question at the back of her mind, "why wasn't Adam at the beach with her, and why did she feel so content without him?" Those are not thoughts she wants to deal with so early in the morning.

Demi awakens more completely now, drawing herself away from her dream and into reality, even if a little reluctantly, and she opens her eyes to see movement between her legs, as Adam is laying between them, shifting her thighs apart to make himself more room on the bed. The hotel sheets they have been sleeping under have been thrown carelessly to the side of her, whether in her slumber, or by Adam, she doesn't know.

He is sprawled out comfortably now between her spread open legs, sliding her panties to the side and exposing her already aching pussy, diving into her sweet nectar, which he had gently been touching and teasing and caressing only moments ago when she had been dreaming. He had been using his soft touch to slowly wake her from her sleep, which explained all those internal feelings and tingling's, teasing and wants she had been experiencing in her sleep.

She lets out a loud half moan, half yawn, but it also carries a sound of enjoyment with it, and she throw her legs open even more, giving him access to all of her, awakening more and more each moment as his tongue works its magic along her wet folds, tasting her. Eagerly lapping up all of her juices. She sits up on her elbows slightly, looking down at him while he pleases her. "I was just dreaming about being on the beach all by myself, toes in the sand, soaking up the sun. I was wondering where you were," she says sleepily with a laugh. "Mmm, I'm right here," he says, his words vibrating his lips against her most intimate of areas, and she can feel it right down to her core, turning her on even more.

    Reaching down, she runs her hand along the top of his head, playing with his hair for a moment, just enjoying the feeling of his warm tongue all over her clit and pushing deeply into her wet hole, tongue fucking her. Then, feeling a bit frisky this morning herself, she asks him to turn and lay with his body over to the side while he eats her out, so that she can please him too, not wanting to be the only one having any fun this morning.

    Upon hearing this, Adam wastes no time doing what she's asked of him, his cock all but jumping at attention the moment she said those words. He had woken up feeling horny as ever, with a rock hard cock that was just twitching and begging for attention. That was why he had crawled between her legs in the first place, needing to start the day off with a good old orgasm or two.

    He moves away from her for a second, sliding out from between her legs so he can take his boxers off, and then he lays his body back down on the bed beside her, but facing the other way, so that his raging morning wood is aimed right at her face, pre-cum already leaking out the tip of it, ready for her soft tongue to devour.

    Then he goes right back to work on her, wanting to please her as badly as he wants her to please him, using one hand to spread her wet pussy lips open wide once more as he licks her slit from top to bottom, making her moan and jump. Pushing his tongue as far inside of her as he can reach, licking up every inch of her.

    Now it's Demi's turn. She reaches out and grips the base of his hard cock in her small hand, giving it a little squeeze before bringing it towards her face and slowly rubbing her wet lips over the head of it, taking her time and teasing him, and now it's his turn to moan out loud. He thrusts his hips forward into her, wanting her, and she opens her mouth wide, letting the head of his penis slip between her lips as she sucks him in, all the way down to the back of her throat. It rubs the back and she gags on it a little, which she doesn't mind at all, then she pulls it back out again and rubs the tip of her tongue over it gently, then her soft lips, lubing him up with her spit while teasing him and driving him crazy.

    He knew that by having woken up this morning with such a hard-on and crawling between her legs while she'd been sleeping, mixed with the way her expert mouth was working his cock, knowing just how to suck and lick him, to tease him and touch him, truly enjoying it herself, that it wasn't going to be long before he blew his load down the back of her throat. But by how well he knew her body too, knowing exactly how to please her, he knew he could have her cumming right there alongside with him in a matter of minutes, it wasn't going to take either of them long to orgasm this morning.

    Adam ran his tongue in circles around the hard nub of her clit a few times, pulling the hood back softly with his fingers and flicking at it gently before sucking on it lightly with his lips and tugging on it with a little more force, driving her crazy, working her up more and more, and she moved her hips and her body closer to him. He felt her moan around his cock, the vibrations pulsing through his dick, now slippery wet and coated from her spit, while her soft little hand wrapped tightly around it, sliding up and down, jerking him off quickly. At the same time, her wonderful mouth kept licking and sucking on the head, running her tongue around it in circles, bringing him closer and closer to the edge.

    He moves his free hand up between her legs and finds her wet slit, slippery from her juices and all of his tongue work. He slides two fingers along her silky folds a few times, coating them in her juices and his spit and getting them nice and wet, lubing them up before gently inserting them inside of her, all the way to his knuckles in one quick push. He slides in so easily, and she cries out loud at his intrusion.

Her pussy walls squeeze and clench tightly around his fingers, and he starts to wiggling them around inside of her, pressing up against her g spot, and then he slides them slowly in and out of her while he continues to suck and lick and tug on her clit with his lips and tongue. Her one leg is now wrapped around his shoulders, pinning him against her and pulling him in to her all at once, as she also gets closer to orgasm, needing to keep him right there, making sure he doesn't stop.

Demi may be about to cum all over his face, but that still doesn't distract her from the cock that's right in front of her, rock hard and oozing pre-cum, the cock that she wants to please and make feel good and orgasm as well. So she grips him a little bit harder and strokes him a little bit faster too, turning her hand around slightly while still sucking and licking all over the tip of it, drool now leaking over her lips and down the side of her mouth as she gags on it occasionally when she slides it all the way back in, stretching her mouth and her throat open wide around it.

Soon they are both humping madly against one another and moaning and crying out for more, unable to get enough, and Adam can tell they are about to cum at the same time, which is just what he'd been hoping for. He picks up speed with his fingers buried deep inside of her, rubbing hard on her g-spot while sucking harder on her tiny nub just as he feels his balls tighten and his cock twitch, and then suddenly he's shooting hot cum down her throat at the same time as he feels her vagina spasm and tighten around him, her pussy clenching hard on his fingers as her juices run down his hand and face. She cries out around the head of his cock, shaking and shuddering while she clings to him.

A few minutes later, they slowly turn themselves around and spoon amongst the scattered sheets, snuggling and kissing and cuddling now that they are both far more awake, but not yet ready to get out of bed. It's a little while later before they slowly start to pull themselves up and head for the shower, washing away their morning fun and getting cleaned up and ready to start their day.

Chapter Four

As they had planned and talked about the day before, the pair do no driving that day, leaving the car totally parked, and they stay put in the city they're in for one more night. Even though they are both so anxious to arrive at their destination, and take some real time to relax for a while, they are edging close to a burnout, and not just a mental one either.

Putting all the emotions that they're going through aside, they are both close to a physical snapping point too, having spent far too much time now keeping odd hours, living in cramped quarters in the car, and always being on the road, nonstop driving all the time. They weren't getting nearly enough physically activity, barely even taking the time to get out of the vehicle longer than food and rest stops some days, or a quick bang against the side of the car. This go go go lifestyle was pushing them both to a collapsing point, and they needed some time to stretch their legs, bodies, and minds, even just for a little while, before they continued on any further. Just a little bit of time to recharge their batteries and give themselves a rest from driving.

That morning, once they've showered and dressed and gotten ready for the day, they find that staying in their hotel room is far too much like being in the car when they're stuck in traffic and not driving somewhere though, even if they're relaxing and ordering in homemade breakfast room service, and able to wander around and stretch their legs. So it isn't long before Adam and Demi decide to go out on an adventure and take in some sights in the city that they're staying in.

"Remember that time we did this a couple months ago?" Demi mentions to him, and they both find themselves reminiscing on another tourist moment they had shared together on a day like this once before. That was back before the heist, and a memory in their relationship that already felt like a lifetime ago, and not just a few months prior to where they are in life right now.

Then they both can't help but share similar thoughts they don't want to mention out loud yet; about how that was a very different time in their lives and how so much has changed between them, and drastically, in such a short amount of time. That was back when things were a lot simpler between them, when they were still in their honeymoon stage together, exploring each other, and things had felt new, fresh, and carefree with one another. They may still be on an intense sexual honey moon high, but there is a lot of extra stress in their life now too, and a lot of baggage that has built up between them. Things that they haven't addressed properly, things that have gone unsaid, and some of those things are beginning to take their toll on Adam and Demi and their relationship as it progresses.

So they get ready, packing some things for the day and then they head out, leaving their hotel on foot. They stop first at a corner store nearby to grab some local maps, so they can make a bit of a plan for what they're going to do. Then they grab some coffee from the coffee shop next to the store and then hike down to the nearest bus stop on the side of the road to get on the next bus.

Before the bus arrives, they hold hands and kiss and simply enjoy the morning, sipping their coffee and relaxing, feeling happy just being together without being rushed, or pressured, being able to enjoying stretching their legs and not having to do any driving, not having to beat traffic or be on any kind of time limit for their next hotel check in, or even their next crime, or robbery.

They spend some time that morning traveling from one attraction to another on the bus and by foot, checking out all the places they find on the maps that look interesting and worth seeing. Then they stop and get some take out lunch from a cute little mom and pop restaurant they spy beside a gorgeous park on their journey, once their stomachs start rumbling and alert them to the fact that they've been so absorbed in what they were doing that they've forgotten to eat.

Adam directs them to an open picnic bench a little ways into the park under a partially shady tree, and they eat slowly while taking in the view and all the sounds around them; the birds chirping, the feeling of the warm sun on their faces, the sound of children laughing and playing, people talking, dogs barking, cars driving past them on the road. Things between them have grown calm once more, they feel relaxed and happy in this moment, without all the pressure of the robbery, or even the kidnapping around them, and being outside in the open, away from the car, from the highway, in the fresh air, away from that crazy life they were living in entirety, helps incredibly.

Adam sighs to himself happily, thinking that it feels like with each and every passing day, and with every single mile that disappears underneath their tires, they grow that much closer to living a normal life together. Once more he finds himself slowly reaching down into his pocket and playing with the engagement ring he's got tucked inside the small lighter pocket in the front, the ring that he carries on his person constantly for safekeeping. The ring that he can't stop thinking about, obsessing over almost.

He slips the first part of his finger up to his knuckle into it a few times, a nervous habit he is already finding hard to break. Adam remembers the first time he saw the ring, tucked back in the far corner of the jeweler's safe, and he'd known right then and there that he had to have it, and make it their engagement ring. He still doesn't know the right way to ask her to marry him, or when, but he knows he doesn't want to miss the opportunity if it presents itself, even if it's giving him the worst anxiety ever. He wonders if every guy whose thinking about proposing to his girlfriend drives himself bonkers like this.

By the time they leave the park, their stomachs are full and they've taken some time to relax and unwind. They are holding hands and walking closely together now, and they're each feeling happy and lighthearted in the moment, all of the tension and stress they've been experiencing far behind them. Their hearts feel light and free. Demi had noticed that Adam had sighed once or twice, but the look on his face had showed sure contentment, and it made her feel good.

Little did she know though, that while they had been gathering things up and getting ready to leave, the thought crosses Adam's mind that they could use another few easy jobs, or at least one real huge one, a big massive score, to keep them steady and set up for the rest of their lives with money. The thought bothers him for a moment, and puts a damper on the way he's feeling, but then it makes him excited to think of pulling off another robbery with her, even though he promised her they would take a break.

They really are going to need a lot more money, especially living how they're living, wanting to be rich and settled and able to travel and buy and do anything they dream of, spending money at will. And other than the fact that they have to acquire that money illegally, or, choose to, this is the perfect life that he simply never thought he'd have. Pockets and bank accounts overflowing with money, the ability to go anywhere in the world that he wanted, with a gorgeous woman by his side, ready to live life with him no matter what was thrown in their paths.

Granted, that life so far may revolve around a kidnapping, which is how he ever even had the chance to meet this gorgeous woman to begin with, and a life of crime, and that wasn't exactly in the original plans of life that he'd thought of for himself when he was younger. But if this was the dice that he'd rolled, and the options that kept appearing in his path, then he was going to play the hand he was given, because Adam was pretty happy with this hand, and couldn't wait to see where it was going to take them next.

Demi finds herself silently thinking about their life together too, and what the future may hold for them, but her thoughts are traveling in a slightly different direction than his. She is feeling very happy and content with where they are in life right now in this moment, and she is ready to just start a life together, a real settled life together, one that doesn't involve any more crime, or crazy chaos. She is done with all of that and is really hoping that once they reach the coast and have had a few days to truly settle in, take some time to relax together and put all of this behind them, they'll be able to breathe a little easier. And then they can sit down and have a real conversation about everything that's transpired over the last few months, and what may lie ahead for them, and make a real, grown up thought out plan for what their next move is going to be.

  At this point, she truly hopes that grown up move involves buying a big beach house somewhere along the coast line, and waking up snuggled next to him every morning, making love while the sun rises up over the ocean and they hear the sound of the waves crashing down on the beach. The smell of coffee brewing in the kitchen, and maybe, one day, the sound of little feet running to their room to greet them.

  She's been doing her own financial thinking for the future, and Demi figures that with the money they have pooled together already, they could invest it properly like boring adults would do had they been working, and they could live a modest, comfortable life that way together without ever having to work full time again. That would give them all the time in the world to explore each other, and their talents and dreams, wants and desires, together and in life. They could work side businesses, get a degree, take up a dozen new hobbies, the skies were really limitless, she thought happily. She was so blessed to have fallen into this life.

  While they make their way on a long stroll back towards their hotel, they're each lost in their own happy thoughts of their future, neither willing to share with the other yet. As they take in the city and the fresh air, they pass by an old abandoned farm house, tucked far back off the road on a private drive, with a bunch of no trespassing signs posted everywhere, and it's almost totally hidden from passing traffic because of a thick overgrowth of bushes and trees blocking the front yard. They almost miss it themselves. It is exactly the kind of house that they both loved, and now neither of them are thinking about their future anymore.

Sharing a glance together, knowing that they're both thinking the same thing, Adam winks at her, and then they have a quick look around them on the street and wait to make sure no one is watching them, and then they head on down the driveway to check the place out.

Once they draw close enough to make it out clearly, they can see that it still appears to be in good enough shape for what they're thinking of using it for, especially after they have a quick peek around in the windows and doors and see that it doesn't even seem to be used often by bums and drifters or partying teenagers. It is totally empty, though dirty, boarded up and deserted, still in fairly decent condition, and it's good and ready for the taking. Adam gives her a little nudge with his elbow, getting her attention, and she smiles and nods back, now confirming what they are both thinking. This house is going to make the perfect place for a little sneaky and exciting play time once the sun goes down and the town grows dark later.

Giggling, they hold hands once more and make their way back down the driveway and out onto the road, taking a quick peek around once more to make sure they still haven't been spotted, and then they begin walking back to the hotel to prepare for their evening. All kinds of kinky thoughts are running rampant in their minds, each of them growing more and more excited as the time passes. Because with this kind of thing, they are still just getting started, and have endless ideas and want to seize every opportunity that comes their way to make the most of them.

Chapter Five

    Demi can feel her heart hammering so hard in her chest that it almost seems like her ribs could burst open at any second, exploding everything inside of her out all over the inside of her jacket. The pounding is a constant roar in her ears, and it's so loud she cannot hear anything else. This feeling of deafness makes her even more nervous than she already is, finding herself on edge, constantly looking around her to make sure no one can see her here in the dark.
    Slowly, walking on shaky legs, legs that feel like they are far too weak to be able to hold her weight, she makes her way up the walkway towards the abandoned house that they had come across earlier. And as she makes her way cautiously, she shivers in the cool night air. It is so dark here behind the thick layer of bushes that she cannot even see the stars in the sky, let alone the street lights and cars that are passing by not too far away on the street. She has a hard time making out the ground in front of her, and she walks extra slowly to watch her footing. Even the sounds here are muffled by the thick leaves and overgrowth, not that she can hear anything over the pounding of her own scared heart anyway. She feels so alone here, so lost in the dark, she may as well be miles away from anyone.
    Finally, she reaches the front porch of the abandoned house and she scales it slowly, carefully, taking her time and holding onto what is left of the railing as she climbs the stairs and makes her way across the porch. She has to be sure not to step on any boards that look unsafe; there are many that are too rotten or about to give way and are dangerous for her to step on.
    Eventually she makes her way safely to the front door, finding it warped and falling off its hinges and already slightly ajar, like the house has been waiting for her, inviting her to come on inside. She has no problems pulling the door the rest of the way open, providing herself

more than enough room to make her way inside of the house, as it gives her zero resistance like she had thought it would, although it creaks and groans loudly on its hinges.

    If Demi had felt like it was chilly outside, it is even colder here inside of the house, the air stale and hidden from any day time sunlight, and she finds her whole body breaking out in a shudder, shivering now out of sheer cold and not excitement or the nervousness of exploring an abandoned house all on her own. Goosebumps break out all the way down her legs, and she shakes a little harder and pulls her jacket that much tighter around her for some extra warmth.

    She steps inside the front doorway and a smell hits her hard, overpowering her, so strong she can almost taste it. It's a dusty smell, or an old, moldy smell, she isn't quite sure what, but it seems to be coming from everywhere and it's certainly not the most pleasant thing she's smelt. It's foul, and fits with the look of the house.

    It doesn't matter how bad the smell is though, because she doesn't plan to be here very long anyways. She's just here for a quick late night adventure, taking some time to explore an old, abandoned house, because it had always been something she had found fun and exciting, and she was extremely grateful that Adam humored her in this crazy past time of hers as well. Once she's done, she is out of here, and going to be heading back to their cozy hotel room to enjoy a couple of glasses of wine, and maybe a hot bubble bath to warm her up from the chill of this place.

    She reaches into the front pocket of her jacket and pulls out the small flashlight that she'd brought with her, bringing it out and turning it on, shining it around and slowly taking in the scene in front of her. She hadn't risked turning it on outside for fear of being seen or caught, but it feels safe enough now that she's inside.

    It takes a moment for her eyes to adjust to the brightness of he flashlight in the dim house, but once they do and she has a look around, she finds she is standing in the front mudroom area of an open concept house, or what is left of it anyways, and although this place is badly decaying and rotting away she can tell one side of this room was once the living room by a moldy old couch pushed up against one wallpaper pealing wall. There are scraps of an old blanket thrown about the room, either chewed on by rats, or moths, or just fallen apart with age over time.

  On the other side of the room she can see a large broken window overlooking the side yard, with an old rotted out high back chair fallen into the corner, and she imagined that once upon a time people would have ate dinner there, looking out over their beautiful gardens, maybe sharing a lovely homecooked meal while talking about their day. There were a pile of broken boards tossed in the corner along that same wall there that she assumed were once nailed up over the broken window, keeping the world shut out.

  She swings the flashlight back around the room again, gripping it tightly in her hands, and Demi realizes that there are really three ways that she can go next as she explores the house, and she survey's her options. She could go forward through the living room and into the kitchen that she can see through the half walled walkway to the left of her. She could go down the hallway in front of her, past the stairs to the right, where she assumes there is likely a main bathroom, maybe some closets and a bedroom or basement access, and possibly a door to the backyard. Or she could go upstairs, where there are likely other bedrooms and bathrooms and rooms to explore.

  A breeze blows past her as a draft comes in from somewhere farther in the house, and it causes her to shiver and pull her jacket in closer around her again, trying to warm herself up a little more. She finds herself wondering if tonight isn't the best evening weather wise for exploring. A few leaves rustle over in the corner with the blowing wind, giving her a little bit of a scare, and it brings her out of her thoughts and back to reality. She decides to get a move on and get on with this, and makes up her mind to start upstairs first. She'll go up the stairs and start with exploring the top of the house and work her way through it to the bottom, and then she can call it a night.

    Demi wanders to the bottom of the stairs and takes a glance up them, aiming her flashing upwards, looking at the state of them. Then she takes her time, making her way up and walking slowly, one hand tightly gripping the crumbling railing for support, the other hand still tightly holding her flashlight, lighting her way. She watches her footing extra carefully, once more hoping that none of the stairs break and give way underneath her as she climbs, or that the handrail doesn't pull free from the wall and she tumbles. She finds herself thinking that the last thing she needs to happen tonight is that she gets injured in here all alone and then has to call for help in an abandoned house with a broken leg. She'd be sure to get slapped with a trespassing charge on top of it all. She lets out a nervous laugh and then forces herself to push those thoughts away.

    She reaches the top of the staircase safely, and takes a long, deep shaky breath, willing herself to calm down. She stops there for a minute to have another look around down the hallway in front of her with her flashlight first, seeing what she's going to check out next.

    There are a handful of doorways that she can see down the hall in front of her; some of the doors to rooms and closets are open and some of them are shut, but it's so dark upstairs without any real windows broken open up here or any light being let through, so it's hard to make anything out. Her flashlight doesn't do a great job of brightening the place up either, only really reaching a handful of feet out in front of her in a dim glow. She should have planned this out more beforehand, and brought a real mag-light with her, something that would have broken up the dark better. This had all been planned on a whim so quickly after passing this place earlier today after lunch.

    There is a moment while she's standing there that she thinks that she can see something, some kind of movement down at the end of the hallway, and at first she would have sworn on it. Demi feels her breath catch in her throat and her palms go sweaty, shaking, making the flashlight jump and dance around her. The problem is, she is too far away down the hallway with her little flashlight to see. Whatever it may or may not be, she'll have to grow closer to make it out, and there's nothing she can do about it standing here. She swallows hard against a lump that's forming in her throat, and tells herself that she's being ridiculous. She didn't see any movement, and she needs to stop scaring herself and get on with her exploring. Being all alone in this spooky house has simply got her on edge, that's all, and her imagination is crazy.

  Demi gives her head a little shake, trying to clear it a bit and refocus on the task at hand, forcing herself to doubt that she'd seen anything at all. She draws in a long, deep breath, and then she slowly begins to make her way down the dark and musty hallway, before stopping at the first door on her right.

  Hesitantly, she reaches out and pushes the half open door the rest of the way open, and it creaks and groans loudly in the silence, echoing around her, sounding like it hadn't been moved in years. She has a listen for a moment for any sounds other that her own hammering heart and gasping breathing, and then she walks carefully into the room.

  It's just a tiny bedroom, with the remains of an old mattress and some garbage shoved into a pile against one wall, and a few of the floorboards have been pried up and pulled lose. There is nothing else in the bedroom, leaving it looking depressing and barren. The window in here is still boarded up nice and tight, making it all but pitch black in the room. All the upstairs windows seems to still be shut up and untampered with by vandals, weather or time, allowing in no moonlight or distant streetlights, and it feels like midnight in here, and farther and farther away from civilization with each and every passing second that she spends there.

  She makes her way back out into the hallway, once more ignoring the movement she swears she sees, or doesn't see, out of the corner of her eye, movement that's just too far away for her flashlight to make out clearly. She tells herself that her brain is simply playing tricks on her, running wild up here in this abandoned house while she's wandering around in a dark and spooky hallway all alone. Her eyes simply can't tell what they are seeing in the dark, and her imagination is limitless, which is a blessing and a curse. She gets stern with herself and demands that she get a grip, because she had wanted to do this after all, this had been her idea. Then she makes her way to the closed doorway across the hall, next on her list to explore.

    She reaches the door and shines her light on the handle as she opens it. This time, Demi finds an old, very smelly bathroom, in serious need of repairs. Or, to be torn down and burnt, she thinks to herself in disgust, just like pretty much the whole house should be at this point, from what she can see and has explored. The smell that hits her nose is the worst smell she's experienced here yet, and she regrets ever opening the door.

    Slowly, she backs out of the bathroom, anxious to get away from that sight and the horrible smell, scrunching her face up and giving the door a good slam behind her. She turns to continue to make her way down the hallway, this time determined to walk a little farther down with the flashlight and show herself once and for all that there is nothing there to be scared of. She needs to pull up her big girl panties and get a hold of herself, and she finds herself wondering what has come over her this time, as she's never felt like this before.

    Suddenly, there is someone standing right there in front of her in the dark, a towering figure looming over her and blocking her way. He shocks her so badly it completely takes her breath away, and any will to scream goes right along with it, leaving her in silenced terror. Demi is then grabbed roughly around her arms, fingers gripping her tightly right through her jacket, holding her still, and the flashlight slips from her hand, falling to the floor, the lens breaking into pieces, leaving them in complete blackness as it rolls away, useless.

    She can just tell that this is a man as his large frame

leans in over hers, causing her to feel helpless, and his breath is hot on the side of her face as he grows closer to her ear. She can smell him too, he smells like a mix of cheap cologne and whiskey, like he'd recently been drinking up here before she'd mistakenly crossed paths with him in the hallway. Then she hears him whisper to her, his voice sounding gruff, breaking the silence that surrounds them, and breaking through her train of thought, making her shudder in his grip. "Now, what's a pretty little thing like you doing in an ugly dump like this? Looking so fine, just ripe for the picking."

Demi is still so startled that this is happening to her, she is so taken aback that she can barely breath, let alone reply to this man right away. She can't even comprehend that this is reality yet. It takes her a moment to suck in a shaky inhale and exhale, and then another to find herself and get her voice back in her control before she responds to him. But then her voice cracks, betraying her false confidence as she speaks. "Please don't hurt me, just let me go. I won't tell anyone that you're here, and I promise I will leave right now. I swear! I was just doing some exploring, and I definitely wasn't looking for trouble."

He must have found some humor in what she said, because he laughs at this, a deep laugh that does something to her in the pit of her stomach, and a tingly sensation she hates to admit she's feeling begins between her legs. Then he wraps one arm tightly around her and slowly starts dragging her down the hallway, down towards the end of it where she had been so sure she had seen movement earlier. She had been stupid to doubt herself, she thinks bitterly. She should have checked first, right away when she thought she had seen something, and then ran while she may have still had a chance. "Well," he leans in once more, interrupting her thoughts, "You have certainly found all sorts of trouble now pretty lady, and I have no plans of letting you go tonight. But I don't think I'll hurt you too much."

Demi tries to fight back against her attacker, and begins to struggle and squirm in his arms with everything that she's got, trying desperately to get away from him but it's no use; he is built far larger and stronger than she is, and has no problems over powering her, controlling her and doing with her what he pleases. He starts pawing at her, grabbing and ripping at her, and then suddenly her jacket is stripped from her body, leaving her shivering.

Then she is roughly shoved up against the wall as they reach the end of the hallway, and the weight of his body is pressing against hers, pinning her and keeping her there. The wall has no give behind her, and his body may as well have been built out of brick in front of her. She is trapped. His mouth finds hers in the dark, and his lips are hot and needy, his tongue pushing its way past her lips, parting them open, forcing his way inside. He tastes just like the whiskey she'd smelt on his breath, and he caresses her own tongue with his as his body begins to grind against hers.

Her resistance continues to weaken the more that he takes control of her, using her as he pleases. She hates to admit it but he is driving her crazy, and as his hands begin to make their way along her body, exploring her over her clothes, she feels her arms drop to her sides as she gives up what little fight against him she had left, surrendering herself up to him. She feels herself turning to putty against him. He laughs at this, that sexy sound again, his laugh vibrating into her mouth and down through her entire body, making her shudder, turning her on, her pussy growing damp between her legs. "That's my good little girl," he says, breaking away from their kiss and whispering once more in her ear, "Let go and give in to me, you know that you want me." Then he slowly kisses and nibbles down her neck, paying attention to all her sensitive areas.

What he's doing to her feels so good already, another shudder breaks out through her body, this one seeming to flow right down to her toes, making them curl inside of her shoes, her stomach clenching tightly in a knot. He already seems to know the best ways to touch her, and please her, in all of the places that she loves the most, and he appears to just be getting started. She can't even imagine what he has planned for her next, and she cannot help but shudder once more, this time in anticipation.

He grabs at the bottom of her shirt, pulling it away from her body as it tugs up against her back, and then she feels his hands sliding up over her stomach, the palm of his hand rubbing roughly against her skin as he begins to explore her. His hands make their way all over her body, touching her everywhere, no part of her seems to be off limits to him as he enjoys her.

Then he grabs at her chest, squeezing her breasts a little bit, and begins pinching her nipples lightly, tugging and pulling on them, making her moan. Then his mouth is all over hers again, silencing her sounds but only for a moment, before moving on to kissing her neck, nibbling on her jaw, and licking along the spots that make her weak, causing her to moan and wiggle her body against him. More and more, she feels herself giving up to him with each passing second, no longer wanting to fight him, or to try and get away, she just abandons her will and lets him take her, letting him make her feel good and have his way with her however he wants. Surrendering herself to him completely.

That feeling of wanting to be totally at his mercy only lasts for another moment though, before his hands make their way from her breasts to her arms, and then upwards until he's grabbing at her wrists, pulling her arms up over her head, still pinning her to the wall with his strong body. She wonders what he is up to, when suddenly her wrists are being yanked together roughly with a rope that was bound above her to the wall, a few feet above her head, and then she's tied that way, the rope holding her arms and hands steady and pinned, while he keeps the rest of her body immobile and still pressed against the wall. Now, she's full of the desire to get away again, even though she's all but helpless now, and it's far too late.

The thought of yelling crosses her mind, but then his mouth is on hers once more, passionately, needing her, hungerly, greedily taking her lips and tongue, forcing his way into her mouth and showing her no mercy. His hands are far more free now to roam with no restrictions, not having to hold her steady, and so he takes his time with her body now. He runs his hands all over her stomach once more, up to her breasts, pulling them from her bra and freeing them, tweaking and pinching her nipples, harder this time, causing her to cry out into his mouth again and again.

He loves the sounds that she makes when she's turned on. He wants to listen to her make them all night long. He wants to hear her cry out in orgasm, in ecstasy. Then he uses his knee to force his way between her legs, spreading them apart and grinding his thigh up against her moist opening, rubbing her with his leg through her pants. He can tell that she's already wet and ready for him, he can feel her heat and her dampness even before he touches her there with his hands.

Demi is totally turning into putty all over again, helpless and completely his for the taking, and a moment later she feels her body give way; if he hadn't have been holding her up, with the rope tying her hands above her keeping her there against the wall, she would have fallen to the floor right then and there, no longer in control of herself. "I've got you," he whispers softly in her ear, "You can let go," and she shivers once more, this time not from the cold at all, but from the excitement of what's happening, and everything she knows is to come.

His hands are making their way around her body again, tracing along her stomach and hips, exploring her until he reaches the waist band of her pants. He takes his time, slipping his fingers inside and tugging on them gently, listening to her moan once more. The sounds she is making are driving him crazy though and he no longer wants to wait. He is quick to undo her pants and yank them down a bit, along with her underwear, leaving them around her knees and totally exposing her to him there in the dark hallway. Then without a moment's hesitation, he slides two of his fingers up and down her wet slit, watching her throw her head to the side and let out a long groan as he coats himself in her juices, finally touching her where she craves him the most.

Her body starts to shake, she is feeling so turned on right now and the anticipation of his teasing is killing her, and he holds her with one hand as he expertly maneuvers his way around her wet pussy, driving her wild. His fingers rub against her little nub, finding her sweet spot, pressing hard and moving in circles around her clit, making her moan and cry out for him, wanting more and more. He moves his mouth back to kissing and nibbling along her neck, finding all of her sensitive spots there again, making his way to her ear lobe and breathing on it lightly before running his tongue along the lobe and nibbling on it. He can feel her torso tense up and shudder beneath him as he drives her absolutely mad.

She could only stand so much of this delicious torture from him before Demi begins bucking wildly against his hand, pulling against her restraints, the rope digging into her skin. She's trying to push herself into him, giving herself up to him and eager for more as he brings her to the edge of an orgasm. She wants to cum so badly. She wants to cum for him.

He knows exactly what he's doing to her and he never lets up, never stops, holding her tightly and keeping her close to his body while his fingers work their magic on her. He rubs her clit in circles, faster and faster, pressing harder on the hood, forcing her orgasm to rip through her, making her tremble right down to her toes, juices leaking down his hand, her moans and cries of passion echoing around them in the dark.

He steps away from her then, leaving her limply laying against the wall, slowing coming down from her orgasm. And while she's glad for the break to catch her breath, it takes her a minute to realize that he wasn't done with her yet. Instead, she could make out enough in front of her to tell that he was taking off his pants, and she could hear the rattle and clang of his belt buckle as he undid it, followed by the sound of his pants falling to the floor. She takes in a deep breath and fights against the feelings raging around inside of her, horniness mixed with uncertainty, and with a shaky voice, she asks him what he was doing. Whether her voice was shaky from fright, or from that powerful orgasm that had just overtaken her, she wasn't quite sure.

It does her no good to ask him though, because he never does answer her. Instead, he just walks towards her once more, closing the distance between them while naked from the waist down now, cock standing straight out in front of him, ready for her, burning desire written all over his face. He grabs her by the arms and spins her around roughly, but not hurting her, the rope turning with her as he forces her into the wall, the old wallpaper musty smelling so close to her nose.

He reaches down and tugs her pants the rest of the way down her legs before pulling them off of her completely, leaving her nude from the waist down as well, her shirt still bunched up over her chest. Then once more, he uses his knee to spread her now sticky legs apart, even wider this time, pressing roughly on her thigh, opening her up and leaning in behind her, grinding against her gently, the head of his large cock brushing against her ass cheeks.

Demi draws in a long deep breath, and once more the smell of the house, now mixed with the smell of sweat and sex, hits her nose, all her senses feeling heightened from the experience. Her pussy is throbbing between her legs in anticipation of what's about to happen to her next. After having his fingers inside of her, she can't help but wonder how his cock is going to feel. Her heart is pounding, her chest shaking, and her palms were balled into sweaty fists held up above her head.

He stands right behind her now, the base of his hard cock gripped tightly in one hand, while he slowly slides it up and down the length of her, teasing her, wetting the head of it with her juices. With his other hand, he reaches down and grabs at one of her ass cheeks tightly, pulling it to the side and opening her up, exposing both of her tight little holes, her pussy glistening wet for him, giving him total access to her.

A cool gust of wind blows down the dark hallway and brushes past them, and he watches her body shiver as the chilly air reaches her wet folds, goosebumps breaking out all over her arms and down her legs. He takes in the shape of her, stretched taunt by her arms held up above her head, legs spread open wide for him. He continues to take his time for a few more minutes, making this last and teasing them both some more. He slowly runs the head of his cock up and down her soaking wet slit, covering him even more in her wetness, feeling the tip make contact with her clit every so often and making her jump, and then he moves upwards and slips past her tight hole, almost being swallowed inside before stopping himself.

He can feel her legs trembling against him now, barely holding her up and vibrating beneath him as she moans and throws her head from side to side, so turned on by his teasing, ready and wanting him, and he knows he isn't going to be able to handle too much more of this himself either. So with one smooth motion he slides his cock all of the way inside of her, filling her hole and stretching her tight pussy wide open, feeling her wet lips clench tightly around his shaft like they're sucking him in, watching his cock disappear.

They both moan in unison this time, but hers sounds like a moan of pure pleasure, finally being filled with his cock like she wants, like she's been craving after being teased and tormented like this. His moan sounds more like an animal growl, something primal, deep from the back of his throat. They both needed this.

He reaches up and holds onto the wall beside her arms for leverage, keeping himself steady and wanting to really pound into her, giving her his all. Then he grabs her tightly around the hip with his other hand, pulling her tiny body into his, feeling his large cock bottom out that much deeper inside of her, right to the brim. Slowly, he starts to slide his cock all the way in and out of her, in long steady strokes, thrusting his hips as he holds her, loving the silky wet tightness of her, wanting all of her, wanting to take her and make this last.

Demi is soaking wet now, she can hear the slippery sounds that they're making echoing all the way down the hallway. Her pussy is on fire; she is ready to cum at any moment, throbbing and aching for him every time his cock leaves her, moaning every time that he fills her completely again. Her juices are starting to drip down his cock now, coating them both, and he has no problem telling her that, although he steps out of character in the scenario they're roleplaying to do so, but she no longer cares.

"Fuck Demi, I just love taking your soaking wet pussy, I love how tight you are, milking me, so fucking juicy all over my big cock. I love making you mine." They are moaning together now, crying out loud in the abandoned house, their cries echoing down the hallway. His hands are all over her body once more, traveling back down and making their way between her legs, playing with her wet folds, spreading them wide and finding her hard clit to play with again, rubbing circles around it while he keeps thrusting into her harder and harder from behind.

Then he leans in close and kisses the back of her neck, and then up along the side of it and over to her ears, nibbling on her ear lobe, breathing into her ear lightly, feeling her whole body shudder beneath him as he knows exactly what she likes. He whispers to her, "mine," before telling her that he's going to cum soon. "Fuck, Demi, I'm about to bust, I want you to cum with me. Cum for me baby, cum all over my big, hard cock."

Demi moans back to him that she's cumming too, she can no longer hold herself back, and then they both explode together, shaking and breathing heavy, bodies thrusting into one another, wet juices dripping everywhere, while he clings to her desperately. Adam keeps fucking her slowly for a few more minutes, while her pussy slowly stops spasming and squeezing him, letting them both come down from their orgasm and allowing their breathing and heart rates return to normal before he stops.

Then, moving ever so slowly because he feels shaky

and rather spent now as well, he reaches up and unties the straps around her wrists, letting her arms fall down and feels her body totally collapse into him, catching her while he spins and pulls her into him, leaning against the wall for support. He starts kissing her everywhere, whispering to her over and over that he loves her while holding her tightly in the cold, dark, deserted house's upstairs hallway.

Chapter Six

After a lazy, slow start to the day the next morning, drinking a few coffees on the balcony and taking in some fresh air, the pair shower, pack up their bags and hit the road once more, heading the rest of the way towards the coast. And a lazy morning is necessary for them after the late night they'd shared together the evening before.

They are both feeling far more rested now, more relaxed and in a much better state of mind than they have been lately, and getting back into the car is easy this morning, especially being so close to their destination now, knowing that they don't have much farther to travel before they can finally park the car for a good long while, and put all of this behind them.

Demi is the one driving this morning, sitting happily behind the wheel, taking in the sights around her and loving the feeling of being in charge, because it gives her a sense of control on when they get to the coast, even if that is a ridiculous thought though since Adam is the faster driver. It's more of a mental thing than anything; in reality, driving just gives her something to do to keep herself and her mind busy instead of going antsy in the passenger seat, wondering how much longer it's going to take to get there, or if they could possibly drive any faster, or take a different route.

Adam seems to be doing just fine sitting there though, but he has been spending the entire drive so far glued to his cell phone, and keeping mostly to himself. When she asked, he told her that he was working on plans for their vacation on the coast; checking out and booking different hotels for them to stay at, researching various activities that they could do together, and local entertainment that would be happening while they were there. He doesn't seem to be up for small talk with her much, so she leaves him to his phone and continues to take in the scenery they pass as she drives.

The truth is though, he hasn't done much of that at

all. For the most part, he has spent the entire trip so far text messaging back and forth with Brandon. The conversation had started innocently enough, Adam had simply thought it might be nice to drop Brandon a line and catch up as he knew Brandon was living right there on the coast where they would be staying, and after the thoughts about another crime had popped into his head last night, he felt like it wasn't quite a coincidence that they were heading to the same place Brandon was right now. He couldn't help but wonder if Brandon might not have any connections they could use.

But once they had started chatting, it had become apparent that Brandon had not only *not* given that lifestyle up, he had moved on to even bigger and better things. Adam had kept the messages private so far because he wasn't sure where this was going to lead yet, and he didn't know how Demi was going to react to him talking to Brandon at all, or the thoughts that were forming in his mind. He wanted to know if this was going to be worth anything before he made a mess with Demi. He knew she still felt pretty sour about him when Adam and her had first left town, and he had told her that he hadn't had any contact with Brandon since.

There was this nagging, constantly lingering thought in the back of his mind that as much as he wanted to just check out, take some time off and relax with her, what he really wants to be able to do is truly do that with her for the rest of their lives, live like they're on a forever vacation, and he wants to be able to do that now. Or as soon as possible. He just doesn't believe that they have enough money stashed away to keep them going the way they want to live, and he wants to see it added to in a massive, almost unlimited amount.

Brandon has mentioned that he's working on a big job right now, a job that he could use some help with, but it would be a robbery this time, and not a kidnapping. It will provide a big, big chunk of cash for all those getting a cut, and it sounds like a damn easy job as well. Especially compared to the last few jobs that they've done with just the two of them, and the lengths that Demi has put herself through to make it all work and come together. Compared to those, this one is going to be a walk in the park, and possibly set them up for good.

But deep down inside, he has to admit that he doesn't think she is going to handle any of this well, and he's scared to tell her until he really has a chance to sit down with Brandon and hash this out more and make a formal plan, so he has something concrete to go forward to her with. Adam isn't going to bring this up and get her upset without first making sure this is a for definite, solid plan thing. Demi keeps talking about wanting to settle down and live a normal life with him, but he can't stop thinking about their future, and everything they have been through already, from the kidnapping to the heist, and what really lies next for them, and how to move forward. And he cannot stop thinking about the ring that's burning a hole in his pocket either.

He doesn't feel confident in how she's going to feel about him asking her to marry him right now, nor does he feel very confident about talking to her about possibly doing another robbery, and especially not with her original kidnapper, someone she's basically forbid him to talk to anymore. But he does feel confident in himself, and that he is making the right choices, and he knows himself too well to think he'd turn down an easy sounding job like this either. He knows that he just needs to find a way to mesh all these things together, because they have to work out for him.

All of this begins to eat at him as they drive towards their final coast destination, and it starts to diminish the great mood he was in when they woke up together this morning, refreshed and recharged from their naughty sexual roleplaying, so ready to hit the road one last time. None of this change is lost on Demi either though, who has not only noticed that Adam seems extremely preoccupied with his phone, not showing her the sights or attractions that he normally does, but that he's also still very shut up and quite, even when she continuously tries to make conversation with him, poking and prodding, which is unusual for him as well. By now he usually cracks when something is bothering him, or when he isn't feeling like himself.

    She can't help but worry about him though, and wonder what it is he's thinking about. A thought that she hates to think about forms in her mind, that maybe he is having second thoughts about taking off on a vacation with her, or if she's done something that bothers him, or if it's their relationship in general. Or maybe, it's something else entirely that she hasn't even thought of yet.

    Because Adam had seemed so on board with taking some time off and having a vacation with her, the thought that he may be stressed about money, or another robbery, or something else along those lines never even crosses her mind. She has been tracking their finances well, even if he doesn't always want to talk to her about it, and she knows that they can live free, and rather lavishly at that, for quite some time before they should start thinking about their finances for the future more seriously. If they invest what they have properly, and make some better choices, they won't have to return to a life of crime and robbery at all, ever again.

    She tries to shake off the emotions, runaway thoughts and doubts about their relationship that she's having as she drives, knowing that once again she is only being ridiculous by running things she doesn't know for sure over and over again in her mind, coming up with different scenarios and situations that aren't real, simply because Adam is being too quiet. The likely hood is that all of this traveling and driving and a life on the road is getting to him, getting to them both, even after they took some time off to rest. They both truly need some quality down time on the beach to recharge and get back to themselves.

    She's determined to refocus her mind on this and keeps driving, now just wanting to get them to their vacation beach hotel, so they can start relaxing and getting back to normal in no time, whatever their normal is. She's just looking forward to finally having a real life with him, and finally relaxing.

Chapter Seven

  Almost as soon as they reach the city along the coast line where they've planned to stay for a while, hitting an open stretch of highway where they can really take in the view of the coast, it's like a switch has been flipped inside of Demi, and it happens in what seems like an instant. All of her worries and cares, all of the stress and tension from the past little while that have been forming in her mind seem to flow right out the window as she lowers it, and the salty breeze from the ocean hits her face and blows her hair out behind her as well.
  When Adam sees the change happen in her, the shift that's so apparent and so quick, he feels a lot of his own worries fly away too, his heart feeling light and happy just as she is feeling. It's contagious. She was right, he thinks to himself, they both do need a break from all of this, because true, relaxed happiness has been really rare in their relationship, and she deserves it. They both do. He vows then and there to make this last robbery worth it, so that he can truly give her the life that he wants to, so that they can leave all of this behind them once and for all.
  The view along their drive right now, as they grow closer to their hotel, is so breathtaking, that Demi is ready to pull over right then and there, right on the side of the busy highway, just to take it all in, feeling overwhelmed by the beauty of it all. Adam can't help but let out a little laugh, so tickled by her eagerness in all of this, enjoying how much she seems to soak up every moment, and he adores how loving and open she is with herself, allowing herself to feel every emotion whenever she's experiencing it, allowing herself to never love or take in too much.
  After few more minutes of watching her drive though, while noticing that she's not always watching the road, Adam can tell she can't contain herself anymore; he's starting to think that if she doesn't pull the car over soon and either take a break or let him drive, she's likely going to cause an accident in her childlike wonder. He tells her,

half jokily, that she's going to drive them into oncoming traffic soon, distracted by her own happiness, and that he's going to GPS them off the highway and navigate them to a side road that will take them right down to the ocean for a better view. Then they can get out of the car and walk down the beach a ways, and take a mini break. From there, he figures she'll either have a chance to get it out of her system for now, or he can take over behind the wheel and she can stare out the window the rest of the way to the hotel.

    Demi can barely get the car pulled over and parked fast enough and then she's out, kicking her sandals off and running down the beach in her bare feet, leaving absolutely everything behind her, totally letting herself feel free in the moment. Adam gets out and stands there beside the car and laughs to himself, watching her, falling more and more in love with her as she runs down the beach. Suddenly, a thought hits him, and he reaches down into his pocket and slides the ring around his fingers a few times, wondering if now might be the right time to propose, out here on the beach, with such a beautiful back drop and both of them feeling so happy and carefree in the moment.

    But then he starts to over think it, growing panicky and getting cold feet, thinking about all the things he's still got planned, especially this robbery coming up that he's thinking about doing with Brandon, and even him talking to Brandon in itself is something he still needs to talk to her about. Things he should probably deal with first, With everything that's going on right now, he's wondering if maybe he shouldn't just wait until after the robbery to propose, when everything is finally said and done. He hates that he is feeling so conflicted and torn over this. He's letting his thoughts and uncertainties spiral out of control, and he needs to make a better plan once they're settled so that he can put his mind at ease. He decides to wait, and so he takes his hand out of his pocket, and starts to follow Demi down the beach.

    Demi can tell that there is still something off about

Adam, something that's bothering him that he isn't talking to her about, but right this minute here on the beach, she refuses to let it bother her anymore. She is far too happy and carefree, and deserves to be right here, right now in the moment, with everything she's ever wanted at her fingertips, her whole life before her and the man she loves beside her.

And deep down inside, she's convinced that Adam is just overwhelmed with the last few months of their lives in the same way that she is, he's just expressing it differently. There has simply been far too much constant on the go living, always driving, staying in road side motels and keeping the worst hours, and not enough normalcy for them to settle into a routine with. They have never lived together in a normal way, experiencing life as a normal couple would.

Plus all the crimes they've committed, being on the run and keeping a low profile from the police and the family they'd robbed is taking a toll on them too. Demi is convinced that they both really need some proper rest, relaxation and sunshine without any driving or timeline to worry about, as well as some damn good slow, passionate sex. Followed up by a whole day filled with hot, kinky explorative sex, and that should set them both right again.

Demi turns around to find Adam slowly walking towards her along the beach. The sun hits her in the face when she turns around, the warmth from it mixing in with the salty ocean breeze, and it all feels so good on her skin, she can't help but inhale deeply as she takes it all in. Then she starts to make her way back towards him too, seeing that he's grown anxious looking a bit, and she takes his hand gently into her own and asks him if he's ready to hit the road again yet, or if he wants to hang out on the beach and rest for a little bit longer with her instead.

There was something in her voice that resonated within him, or maybe it was the way that she squeezed his hand in her own, tight and warm and comforting, but he's quick to snap himself out of the conflict that is going on in his head, and he brings himself back to her, right here on the beach.

Adam takes in a deep breath himself, feeling the ocean air fill his lungs, refreshing him. It does feel good to be here in the sunshine with her. He glances over at Demi, taking her in, watching her eyes smile as she smiles back at him, and he sees that little spark glimmer in the corner, as her smile changes, and he realizes exactly what she's thinking about.

"Why," he says, finally answering her question, smiling back at her and giving her that look he knows she loves. "Did you have something else in mind besides driving?" Demi doesn't say another word to him though, she knows exactly what she wants right now, and she knows he wants it too. Instead, she just squeezes his hand a little tighter, and then gives it a little tug as she starts walking, encouraging him to follow her.

Demi leads them off, down the beach, towards a little outcropping of rocks that gives them a little privacy from the road and from any other beach goers, hidden from sight. Maybe they both need to get one last quickie out of their system before they keep driving and finally reach their hotel.

Adam follows behind, holding her hand but letting her guide them to a spot she likes. He knows better than to question things now; his little vixen is just as horny as he is, and always seems to want to take advantage of every moment they can find to be together sexually, and to please one another. And he doesn't mind one bit.

They don't share any chatter along the way, though it doesn't take them more than a few minutes to reach the boulders that Demi had been thinking about hiding behind. When they do, she turns her head slightly and winks at him before giving his hand a little tug and giggling. Then she picks up the pace and almost skips around the rock cropping, and Adam lets out a little laugh himself, loving her eagerness.

As they round the outcropping it dawns on Adam that they hadn't thought to bring a blanket or anything for them to lay on, but suddenly Demi lets go of his hand and turns, dropping to her knees, smiling up at him wickedly, and he realizes that they won't need one. What's a little sand going to do to harm them, anyway?

While he's thinking this, Demi's already grabbing at his pants, tugging at them, and he feels himself starting to grow hard at her urgency. It always turned him on to see how badly she wanted to please him.

Demi definitely wastes no time, she'd been feeling a mixture of pure excitement and horniness since they'd reached the coast line, and she definitely needs to get it out of her system. She can already feel how wet she is between her legs, sitting on her knees in the hot sand, patiently waiting for her turn after she pleases him first.

She pulls his belt off completely now and his pants drop to the sand, and she gives his boxers a quick tug too, making sure they follow. She looks up at him once more, making eye contact with him as she runs her hands up his bare thighs, his coarse hair tickling against her palms. Adam loves staring down at her like this, and feels his cock twitch in agreement, eagerly awaiting her warm mouth to enclose around it.

Her hands slowly make their way closer to his semi-hard cock, and he lets out a little moan and bites his bottom lip as he reaches down and runs his fingers through her hair. He doesn't apply pressure, doesn't rush her, but he sure can't wait for her to get started, either. Her teasing always drives him wild.

Gently, Demi takes the base of his dick in her hand, giving it a little squeeze, then she leans forward and gives her lips a quick lick first, getting them nice and wet, before she lets the head of it trace ever so slowly along her closed mouth. He moans a little louder now, and his member twitches again, growing that much harder in her expert hand.

Ever so slowly, loving teasing him and being in control like this, loving pleasing him, she gently reaches up with her other hand as well, and starts to stroke both hands up and down the length of him, feeling him growing firmer with every stroke. Demi never moves her mouth away, nor does she open it either, she just keeps teasing him with her lips while lightly rubbing the palms of her hands up and down, and up and down again.

All this teasing is driving him wild. Adam is fully hard now, his cock dripping pre-cum and he is dying to feel her lips wrap around him. Demi doesn't disappoint him, but she teases him just a little bit longer, opening her lips just enough to snake the tip of her tongue out and lightly lick it over the end of his cock, tasting the saltiness of his pre-cum.

Adam leans his head back and lets out a groan at this, and his fingers twitch in her hair, pushing just a little bit, desperate for her now. Slowly, Demi opens her mouth, squeezing the shaft of his cock with one hand to hold him still, then gently she licks her tongue around the head in circles, following with her wet lips, started to suck on the head of his cock ever so softly.

Then she moves her tongue lower, starting to lube up his shaft with her spit, dragging her tongue along the length of the bottom of it, and then back up along the top. The slippery feeling of her tongue mixed in with the tightness of her fist slowly stroking him up and down feels amazing.

She takes her time, teasing him and making sure he's nice and wet, feeling his rock hard cock twitch and the veins pop under her soft touch. She looks up at him while she does this, but he's not even looking down at her anymore. This feels so good, Adam's in heaven, with his head tilted backwards, eyes half closed, just loving the sensations of her soft wet lips and tongue all over him. Knowing that what she's doing is turning him on immensely, she picks up speed, squeezing him a bit tighter with her fist as she strokes him up and down, and finally opens her mouth all the way and lets his penis slip down her throat.

The moment the head of his cock brushes the back of her throat, and he feels her throat tighten around him as she gags a little bit, his eyes widen in attention as he drops his head back down to watch. Demi loves to please him, and he loves to watch her, especially as she'll do anything to make him feel good, and to make him cum.

She stares back up at him, eyes wide, mouth open even wider, letting his cock slide in and out. She keeps her tongue flat, and moves forward on her knees, keeping her head tucked back as well. At the same time, she keeps moving her hand up and down his shaft, faster and faster, and she uses her other hand to reach underneath and lightly cups his balls, feeling them tighten in her gentle palm.

Adam thought he was in heaven before, but he's even more so now, looking down at her while she sucks and deep throats his cock, fisting his shaft and playing with his balls at the same time, a string of drool leaking out of the side of her mouth. "Mmm, fuck," he mutters under his breath, his fingers digging into the top of her head, pulling on her a little bit, pushing her face harder against him. "You give the most incredible blow jobs. I love your lips, your tongue. I'm going to cum in that pretty little mouth of yours."

Demi smiles up at him around his large member, another bit of drool leaking out of the side of her mouth as she does, before she picks up speed, forcing his cock further down her throat with every thrust, gagging on it louder and louder as it keeps brushing the back of her throat.

At the same time, Adam can feel her fingers lightly touching and caressing his balls, tugging on them as they tighten. Her other hand is covered in spit, and giving him the world's slipperiest hand job, keeping the pace with her mouth as she works him, in and out, up and down.

He isn't going to be able to take too much more of this before he cums, and she knows it. She never stops with her mouth or her hands, twisting her fist around his shaft, running her tongue along the bottom of his cock, gagging on the head of it, her throat constricting around it again and again. Adam lets out a loud moan, totally oblivious to the fact that they are still in a public place in the middle of the beach in the sunshine of the afternoon, barely hidden by a pile of rocks. At this point he no longer cares if the whole word hears him.

"Yes, mmm yes Demi, suck my cock," he moans to her once more, dirty talking to her but mostly just letting it all out, squeezing her head and holding her tightly to him and giving in to the sensations and the way she's making him feel while she expertly pleasures his throbbing cock.

Demi can feel him starting to harden even more in her hand and in her mouth, and his cock twitches as his balls tighten in her palms as she pushes him over the edge. His orgasm over takes him, causing his whole body to tremble, his eyes to close as his head falls back, and he grips her hair tightly, holding her face against him as he cums hard, his cock erupting down the back of her throat.

She feels hot spews of cum coat her mouth, her throat, her tongue, and she keeps going for another moment, though very lightly, letting him finish and making sure she's licked every drop clean before she slowly lets his cock slide from her mouth. She stays there on her knees, looking up at him with a smile, wiping the corner of her mouth as he looks down at her with a big, goofy grin on his face, very satisfied, his cock still half hard, slowly catching his breath.

"That was amazing babe," he says, reaching out a hand to help her to her feet, but she playfully shoves his hand to the side, and drops down to her ass on the sand, laying backwards slowly while propping herself up on her elbows, and she slides her legs out to the side, her ankles on either side of his own legs, opening herself to him.

She raises her hand, beckoning him with her finger, telling him, "it's my turn now," and giving him a wink. Despite the sand, he's happy to oblige, dropping down to his knees with her right there on the beach, eager to please her next.

Chapter Eight

A few hours later, with Adam now behind the wheel, he pulls their car into the parking lot of their destination hotel, just a little before dinner time. He has been driving since they finished up their little beach quickie and got themselves back on the road. He could tell that the scenery and the fresh air, mixed in with a few amazing orgasms, was still all too much for Demi to take in, so he had hopped back into the driver's seat once they hit the highway. There was something beautiful and relaxing in the way she took everything in and allowed it to flow through her.

Demi had done some traveling in her life, but never to places like this, places that she had picked and where she really wanted to be, and she also hadn't been out this way along the coast line since she'd been a young child. Most of the traveling she had done in her life had been with her family when her father was still alive, or when she was traveling with a group of friends from college. It hadn't been on her terms, totally free to do whatever she wanted, to soak up every moment and enjoy it at her own pace, with the money and the freedom to live however the hell she wanted.

Plus, having this opportunity to be here with Adam, someone she was so incredibly in love with, who loved her back, who she had nonstop fun and excitement with, never mind the sexual excitement she had with, was amazing. She got to share every moment of this fabulous life with someone by her side. They had unlimited opportunity and endless possibilities in front of them, and their whole lives to spend together. She was on top of the world.

They may have traveled the rest of the way to the hotel in quiet silence, each of them lost in their own thoughts as the car speeds down the highway, but Demi never lets go of his hand the entire drive, squeezing him tightly on occasion and lightly rubbing her thumb up and down along his. She's so content and relaxed, and satisfied, breathing the ocean air in deeply, smiling all of the way to her eyes as she looks out over the ocean.

She's feeling happy in the moment, but Adam is having a hard time controlling the rollercoaster of emotions that's swirling around inside of him, and that's why he keeps his mouth shut. She is so beautiful, and so damn good to him too, and he's so happy to finally be here with her, but he's so conflicted inside himself about how he feels, about planning an upcoming robbery and confronting her with it, and about asking her to marry him. The sneakiness and guilt are eating away at him. He needs some time to make a plan and settle his mind.

Once Adam gets the car parked and they get themselves checked into the hotel, they head to their room to settle in and unpack. They are both starving, but since they are finally here and ready to start their vacation right, they forgo ordering hotel food up to their room and instead, they jump into the shower, getting cleaned up and dressed and ready for a well-deserved night out, finally getting to spend some downtime together and to start to relax.

Adam uses his phone to search around on the internet and finds a fancy restaurant for them to dine at that's not too far from where they are staying. He sits over by the corner of the room on the armchair while he searches, hoping that he doesn't seem obvious, but every time he picks up his phone he panics that Brandon may have text him, or may still text him at any moment, and he prefers to sit where Demi can't see his screen. With every passing moment, he doubts what he's getting himself into more and more, and has to keep reassuring himself that he's just seeing what his options are.

It takes him a few minutes longer than he'd like, but he forces his head back in the game and finds a few places, and shows her the menus. Once they've picked a place, they head out to eat, vowing to let go of everything and live a little tonight, to relax and just enjoy each other, and they order all of their favorite things to eat, and drink just a little too much, forgetting about everything they've been through for a while.

Demi has no problems with any of this, having been looking forward to this vacation with Adam for a very long time. She is ready for everything she's been dreaming about, and then some. But she still can't help but feel like Adam isn't 110% on board with her here, and wonders once more if it isn't something more than just all the traveling and driving and nonstop living on the go that they have been doing that's really getting to him.

They've finally arrived here at their beach destination, and it's time for a much needed vacation. They're done with everything for a good long while, they haven't even spoke about their next move yet, only knowing that they needed time off to relax more than anything. She wonders why he just doesn't seem as happy as she is in the moment, why he can't seem to let go and relax, even though he tells her he is fine. Maybe the reality that this is all over for now just hasn't hit him yet, she finds herself thinking, or maybe there is something else going on that he is hiding from her or just not talking to her about yet. She hates that she feels this way, and forces herself to brush the nagging thoughts aside and to get back to her happy, relaxed feeling for the night.

He's trying really hard tonight, but now that they are finally here in LA, Adam is feeling more and more pressured, going back and forth between the two biggest causes of stress in his mind. The largest part of his stress is coming from the ring that's sitting in his pocket right now. He is dying to get down on one knee and propose, and for her to say yes. Hell, part of him wants to do it right now, right here in this busy restaurant. He wants to see her wearing that ring, and wants to know for the rest of their lives that she'll be his. The problem is, he still doesn't know deep down in his soul what she will say, especially when she finds out what he's been up to, planning another robbery with Brandon behind her back.

Which leads to the whole Brandon issue in entirety, which is also driving him bananas, and the second cause of all of his stress. Now that they are finally here in the city, his phone has been going off nonstop with text messages from Brandon, and it's impossible not to be distracted by that. They have plans to meet up in the next few days so that they can go over everything in person, hash out all the details and sort out exactly what he is supposed to say to Demi. And that seems to be something he cannot get out of his mind either, or figure out what to do about.

He truly has no idea what she is going to say about this robbery, and that terrifies him. It's not just the robbery at all, they've done enough of those, and that last one was a bit of a dozy, so he doesn't worry what she'll think about actually committing a robbery with him. It's everything else about it, and how he feels like he is going behind her back with this whole thing, cheating on her almost, with secrets, and a secret agenda, and it leaves a yucky feeling in the pit of his stomach. He hates lying to her, and keeping things from her, and every time he does it always blows up in his face.

They are supposed to be here, checked out from everything and relaxing in each other's company, she wanted this so badly, and the last thing he wants to do is ruin their vacation together, or their lives together. He just needs to find a nice, soft, easy way to tell her that they definitely need at least one more big, massive score if they want to be set for the rest of their lives, and he knows a good opportunity when he sees one, even if it does involve someone she hates, and doesn't think he has any contact with.

The weight of all of this is lying heavily on his shoulders, and no matter how hard he tries to turn it off for her tonight and let it all go so he can enjoy the moment, he feels like he is drowning in his thoughts more and more, and he can't escape them. The stress is simply becoming too much for him, and he becomes more and more distracted and withdrawn.

As the night rolls on, Demi watches Adam pick at his food, pushing it around on his plate more than he's actually eating it, and the happy to be on vacation and carefree mood between them starts to fade. They make limited small talk now, even though Demi keeps trying, and now Demi can tell for sure in her soul that something has changed, she just can't figure out what it is. She asks him one more time if everything is alright, her voice shaky and cutting through his thoughts like a knife, but all he does for a minute is reach across the table and take her hand in his.

"I'm sorry babe, I'm just really tired," he says at last, feeling terrible for lying to her, the guilt eating away at the pit of his stomach, and he can taste bile creeping up the back of his throat. "I honestly can't wait to just get caught up on some real sleep and lay around on the beach with you, and stare at you in your tiny bikini. At this point, a good night sleep can't come quick enough." This calms her nerves quite a bit, even though it leaves Adam feeling even worse, and she gives him a big smile, all the way to her eyes once more as the tension leaves her face, and she tells him that she cannot wait to do just that, and soak up some happy vitamin D with him, both kinds.

Adam gives her a laugh and the mood shifts between them once more. They finish up and pay for their meal, and then head out into the night, the ocean air a refreshing change from the restaurant. They hold hands and take a walk out on the boardwalk for a while, leaving their car parked at the hotel and stretching their legs. They don't talk much while they are out by the beach, but the mood between them is a little lighter now, as Demi's mind has been set as ease and Adam is trying his hardest to contain himself for her.

Demi snuggles into his arm as they walk, and Adam holds her close, pulling her into him to keep her warm and feel her tight body pressed against him. They dream about the future while they walk, and what it holds for the both of them, Adam hoping and praying that everything goes smoothly without a hitch, and soon they'd be damn near billionaires at that point, married and happy and set up for life.

Chapter Nine

    The next morning Adam wakes up feeling sluggish and worn out. His head hurts, there is an awful, foul taste in his mouth, and he feels like he's been beaten with something while he slept. He could almost be getting sick, or be hung over, except that he didn't drink last night, and he has a pretty good idea that this is all mental. He's finally starting to feel the strain and pressure of everything he's putting himself through, and he knows that this is only going to reflect back on their vacation, and their relationship as well.

    He lays there for a few more minutes in thought, and then decides that he needs to actually check out from all the things floating around in his head and give it all a break, at least for a little while, so that he can take some time and just be with Demi in the moment, and enjoy their vacation like they're supposed to be doing. Like he promised her they would do. He's starting to feel like some of the tension that's between them is because he is focusing so much on the robbery that he's planning, sneakily at that, and not being present with her like he's supposed to be. He may be desperate to make solid plans and finalize what he's going to do going forward, but it would do them both some good for him to take at least one day and focus solely on her and their life.

    Even though it's early, he rolls over in bed and snuggles up to her for a little bit, holding her close to him, nuzzling her and kissing her shoulders and back lightly until she starts to stir. He doesn't stop touching her, kissing her ever so gently until she wakes up fully, turning over and cuddling him back, loving waking up in his arms.

    They stay this way for a little while before slowly rolling out of bed, but neither of them are ready to start the day yet, finally waking up for the first real time without anything to do, without anywhere to be, with no agenda in mind at all. They order breakfast to their room instead, and make their way out onto the balcony to relax for a while, to eat and drink coffee while they sit and look out over the ocean.

There isn't much talking between them this morning, but the mood is light and happy, so they sit in quiet joy, emptying cups of coffee and lost in their own thoughts, holding hands and taking in the view in front of them. With the brisk ocean air in his face feeling so refreshing this am, it's a wonderful way to wake up, and Adam doesn't find it hard to stay present in the moment and leave the things that he's struggling with behind, at least for a little while.

And Demi is so lost in the beauty of the scene in front of her that she can't imagine doing anything else with her life right now than being here on this hotel balcony with Adam. She can picture the two of them owning a beautiful little home here somewhere, right off the beach like this, overlooking the ocean, and she wants to spend every day waking up, enjoying coffee and the sunrise and starting the morning off with Adam just like this.

She was so content that she could have spent all morning lost in her thoughts, but she was brought back to reality by the feeling of Adam's foot nudging hers from side to side. She forces herself to tear her gaze away from the ocean, and she turns her head to find him staring at her, leaning close to her over the table, his face and lips only inches away from her own.

"Whatever it is on your mind that's got you thinking so heavily right now, smiling or not, I want you to put it on hold," he says to her huskily, "because I have some other things you should be thinking about for a little while instead." He gives her that charming half smile she loves so much, and then he leans in and kisses her, very slowly to start, but tenderly, and with building passion. His hands reach up and gently rub up and down her arms, along the outside of her housecoat. He starts awakening all of her senses, causing a tingling sensation to break out throughout her body, right down to the tip of her toes, making them curl up in excitement.

When he finally pulls away and breaks from their

kiss, she is left dizzy and breathless, so it takes her a minute to find herself, but she never did lose her own train of thought in the process like he had asked. "You may have liked what I had on my mind you know," she says, biting her lower lip slightly, still staring at his lips, "But I can definitely save it for another time if you want to give me more of those kisses to think about instead." She follows that up with a laugh, still feeling a little dazed from his first toe curling kiss.

Adam lets out a laugh with her, and then he stands and takes her hand, pulling her up to her feet to stand with him. Then he kisses her again on the balcony, this time while they're really overlooking the ocean, feeling the breeze flow through their hair, completely on display for anyone who happened to be looking their way while they shared an early morning heavy make out session. Adam holds her steady, pulling her robe open and running his hands all over her body while he makes love to her mouth with his own, passionately, needing her.

The wind is just a touch too chilly for them to be outside naked this am though, so after a few more kisses they slowly make their way back inside of the hotel room, throwing the balcony door shut behind them, never letting go of one another the entire time. They clumsily stumble their way to the bathroom, still kissing all the way, stripping each other of their pajamas as they go. By the time they make it to the bathroom, they're both naked, and ready for a little shower fun.

Adam breaks away from their kiss only briefly, so that he can turn around and start the shower for them to climb into. Demi can't help but watch and stare, biting her lip once more as Adam bends over, his toned backside looking so yummy, his legs exposing all sorts of strong muscles that she can just never seem to get enough of. She finds herself thinking that not only is he so damn handsome, but that she's pretty lucky to have him in her life as well. He's so good to her.

Adam turns back around a moment later and catches her looking at him with love and affection, and he eagerly pulls her back into him again, wanting to feel her lips on his once more, wanting to love her, devour her, taste her. His tongue makes its way into her mouth for one more deep kiss before he pulls away again, and he steps into the shower, and pulls her in behind him.

Once they're under the warm water, and they've had a chance to adjust, Adam grabs her around her arms and pushes her up against the shower wall. She's expecting another kiss, but he drops to his knees instead, the water from the shower head cascading down his back, and he forces her legs apart, opening her wide. She leans back against the wall and props one of her legs up on the ledge beside her, providing herself more support and giving him access to all of her as well.

Adam wastes no time eating her delicious pussy like he'd been craving now that it's right in front of him, all his for the taking. With warm, needy lips he starts to suck gently on her folds, licking her lightly, running his tongue along her slit, teasing her and feeling her body start to respond to him, tasting her juices as they begin to coat his tongue.

He takes one hand, reaches up and uses a couple of fingers to spread her slippery lips wide open, exposing all of her, and now that her clit is poking free he lightly rubs his tongue around it a few times, listening to her moan before he pulls it between his lips, sucking on it ever so gently.

His teasing oral assault on her is driving her crazy. Demi needs more. She is in ecstasy already this morning, unable to get enough of him, or his mouth, fingers and tongue, so turned on by him, so horny for him. Still supporting herself with her legs, she reaches down and grabs Adam around the back of his head, running her fingers through his hair and pulling his face in closer to her. She grinds her clit into his lips and tongue and mouth as he brings her closer and closer to orgasm. She moans out for him, letting him know that she's going to cum soon, crying out for more.

He finally uses his hands on her like she loves, and

slides two fingers deep inside of her, wiggling them around, pressing them in as deep as he can, rubbing her g spot and feeling her tight walls squeeze against his fingers. He runs his tongue around her clit, sucking on it, flicking over the tip of it at the same time, and he can feel her whole body begin to tense and shake as he pushes her over the edge.

Demi cums hard, all but vibrating against him, and she almost loses her footing as her legs shake and her foot that she's got propped up on the ledge slides around on the slippery surface. Adam holds her steady, his own knees on the porcelain tub, hands gripping her thighs tightly as hot water flows down his back and she grinds her wet pussy into his face, bucking hard.

Adam's in a mood this morning, so he never stops. Even though she cries a few halfhearted protests and tries to push him away, he keeps pressing and rubbing on her g-spot, and sucking hard on her clit at the same time. Demi's hands leave the back of his head, and one grabs at the shower curtain while the other clings to her chest, lost in the feelings he was giving to her. A second orgasm isn't far behind her first.

She's moaning louder and louder now, no longer trying to make him stop. He can feel her tight silky folds squeezing around his fingers as he slams them in and out of her wet hole, pounding into her g-spot roughly with them, applying more and more pressure before pulling away each time, driving her wild, his tongue still lapping circles around her little nub, pulling it between his wet lips.

Demi screams out his name, giving into the second orgasm that's ripping through her body, tingling waves rushing through her as her lower body tightens and then explodes. Her pussy clenches around his fingers, squeezing him, holding him tightly like a vice as wetness pours out of her while she cums. Adam keeps fingering her roughly, licking and sucking up every last drop, using his other hand to spread her slippery pussy folds wide, exposing every last inch of her to his eager lips and tongue.

He waits for her to come down from her high, waits until she's stopped spasming around his fingers, and then he pulls his hand away gently, and pulls his face away from between her legs. He gets to his feet and then helps her to stand with both of her feet in the tub once more, although she's still light headed. He holds her for a minute, spinning them around so that she's under the water and has a chance to warm up, and she simply clings to him, relaxing, feeling his hard body pressed up against hers, and his hard-on poking into her stomach. He isn't done with her yet, he's just giving her a little bit of a break for a moment, letting her feel safe and secure in his arms.

Once she's begun grinding those wet hips of hers all over him though, letting him know she's ready again, it starts driving him crazy, and he's had enough waiting. He spins them around again, sliding them towards the back of the tub once more, and she's quick to put her leg back up on the side, her other leg this time as now her back is to him. She grabs onto the wall for leverage, bending herself over slightly and opening herself up, presenting her aching, glistening hole to him.

Adam bites his lower lip, letting out a little moan of anxiousness, and then he grabs his throbbing cock around the base, stroking it slowly, before closing the gap between them. His thighs rub against the back of her legs, his wet hair rough against her smooth skin. He places one hand on the wall beside hers, leaning in, and still with his other hand on his cock he traces the head along her slit, lightly, getting himself nice and lubed up before thrusting all the way inside of her in one quick movement.

Demi lets out a loud moan, arching her back and throwing her hips into him, forcing his cock to slide a little bit deeper inside of her. He holds her around the waist with his now free hand, gripping her tightly, allowing them to adjust to his large cock filling her for a minute before sliding almost all the way out of her tight hole, the lips of her pussy feeling like they're sucking on the head of his cock, before ploughing back into her again, and then again.

It hasn't even been long since Demi's last two powerful orgasms, but she can tell another one won't be far behind it by the way he is fucking her, taking her, filling her with his hard cock, slamming into her over and over, his cock spreading her wide open each time. She is pinned against the shower wall while he holds her steady around the hips with one hand, his body thrusting into hers while the hot water still rains around them. The head of his cock keeps banging into her, hitting all the spots inside that make her squeal.

She can tell it isn't going to take Adam long to cum this morning either. He was rock hard when they started all this, climbing into the shower with her with the head of his cock already dripping pre-cum, and he is breathing in short, ragged breaths now, squeezing her tightly, his fingertips digging into her while he pins her in place, fucking her roughly, slamming her into the shower wall again and again.

Using both hands, she begins to push her body away from the wall each time, matching his thrusts, slamming her ass into him when his cock pushes all the way inside of her, her pussy spreading wide to swallow his cock, and they both moan in unison as her wet hole engulfs his throbbing hard member.

Demi starts panting and moaning as he fucks her faster and harder, and he leans down and licks along the length of her earlobe, making her shiver, before whispering in her ear, "Cum with me baby," She hears his voice and her body reacts on its own, trembling, vibrating, and he feels her pussy start to squeeze and tighten around his penis. He thrusts into her harder, one last time, pushing her over the edge.

They come together there in the shower, Adam with his strong arms around her tiny body, holding her close as she starts to shake and shudder against him. He can feel her tight, dripping vagina squeezing him like a vice, her walls so wet and silky, milking him, clenching hard on the shaft of his cock as he explodes inside of her, the wet, sloppy sound of their fucking echoing in the bathroom.

He glides his cock slowly in and out of her a few more times, letting them both relax and their breathing return to normal, before he slides out of her gently and turns her around, kissing her slowly. He pulls them back under the flow of the water to warm up once more, holding her tightly for a moment, loving the feeling of her small body against his larger frame.

After a little while they take turns washing up in the shower, helping one another with soap, and he helps wash her hair, something she loves and has always found super romantic that he does for her. By the time they're done, they both share a laugh, grateful for the abundance of hotel hot water.

It's a happy start to their day, and they get out of the shower feeling lighter, kissing and sharing "I love you"s, basking in the moment and excited for the beginning of their vacation.

Chapter Ten

Adam and Demi spend the rest of that day simply relaxing and enjoying their time together, living the dream vacation life that Demi has been dreaming about for them for so long. They take what they need with them for the afternoon and then hike down to the beach, just lounging around and soaking up the sunshine, getting their tan on, catching a nap, cuddling, eating snacks and having a few drinks, reading books and swimming in the ocean.

It feels really good to finally just breathe, relax and be together, spending some time living a normal vacation life, checked out and unwinding from everything that they've been through lately. It doesn't take long, a few drinks and a little bit of sunshine later, before Adam finds himself forgetting all about the upcoming robbery he's planning and everything he's been up to behind her back that goes along with it. The guilt and tension that he's been harboring seem to just wash away, leaving him feeling relaxed and able to really be there in the moment with her.

Everything seems to be so light and carefree between them today, everything feels so easy and natural, and happy. Their romance and need for each other is through the roof, and neither one can seem to get enough of the other. They can't seem to keep their hands to themselves, constantly kissing, touching, cuddling, needing one another desperately even after all that incredible shower sex to start off their day. It doesn't even matter to them that they're laying out in the open in public, in the middle of the beach in the middle of the day.

It almost feels like the beginning of their relationship all over again, except without living out of a car and road side hotels, and being on the run from a recent kidnapping, unsure of what to do next. Now they're simply free, relaxed and together, with nothing to do next, and it feels amazing. Demi smiles to herself, thinking that she just couldn't be any happier in the moment.

Eventually the day wears on, and by mid-day they

find themselves curled up on beach towels, sharing a snack and a drink, as conversation leads to talk about them, and their relationship and what they've been through and what the future might hold. For the first time, they sit and have a civilized conversation about the heist, and her involvement with the jewelers wife, feeling comfortable enough to finally approach the subject, not being trapped in a car, or a hotel, with nowhere to turn if things went sour.

Demi feels herself let out a sigh of relief to finally get everything she'd been feeling, all the emotions she'd been harboring and things she'd been stressing about off her chest and out in the open. She'd been holding back so many feelings, and so many concerns and what ifs, and it had truly been eating her inside and out. She had never felt bad about sleeping with the wife, but she had felt guilty that she *hadn't* felt bad, and had actually enjoyed it. She was terrified how that would make him feel, or if he was jealous, or if maybe he would have trouble trusting her going forward.

Adam had never once been upset about what she had done, and in fact had always encouraged it from the beginning, and he reminds her of this. He hugs her tight while she lets out what she's feeling, grateful that they can move on and put that behind them. "Demi, I love you inside and out. And nothing is ever going to change that. I don't even think about what happened that night anymore, and I certainly don't lose any sleep over it, so you shouldn't either."

They snuggle together happily, both of them breathing easier, glad to have all of that built up tension gone and out of the way. Then the conversation changes from what they've been through to what they are going to do next, not necessarily physical where to next plans, but plans for their relationship. Adam feels a spark of hope grow inside of him as he thinks about what he's got planned for their future, and in this happy moment they've created, he feels confident that things are going to work out perfectly for them. She talks lightly about buying a big home somewhere along the beach, and living a life just like they are right now.

As time has passed that day, and the conversation progressed, Adam's made a decision to hold off on proposing to Demi until he's figured out his plans with Brandon for the robbery, and had a chance to sit down and explain it all to her and talk to her about it first. He tells himself not to doubt that anymore. He's convinced himself that because everything is so relaxed and easy between them now, that once he's ready, talking to her will be just as easy, and he'll be able to show her that they need this one last job with Brandon to really get them set up for the life that they're talking about now. And once that's out in the open, he won't be holding any guilt or secrets from her anymore, which will make proposing to her that much easier on him.

And he's also got himself convinced that when he finally does get around to asking her to marrying him, that she's going to say yes. He doesn't doubt that anymore either. He feels in his heart that they're just too happy, and too much in love, for her to say otherwise. He drops a few hints at it while they talk, laying there on a shared beach towel overlooking the ocean, watching the birds fly in the sky above them and children laughing and playing in the waves, taking it all in.

He mentions what it would be like to really live here like she had said a few minutes before, be married and settled and maybe have kids of their own one day, taking them down to the beach to suntan and play, build sand castles and teach them how to swim. They'd have a nice house and do whatever normal people do when they settle down with their lives.

Demi snuggles up to him while he talks, and with the hand that's not tucked around her, holding her close to him, he reaches down into the zippered pocket of his bathing trunks and fingers the ring he's still got tucked inside, imagining what it's going to be like to get down on one knee and ask her to spend the rest of her life with him, picturing the look on her face, and her reaction.

Demi laughs gently, interrupting his train of thought, and he loves the sound as it brings him back to the here and now, laying out on the beach with her, watching the waves, soaking up the sun, feeling her warm tiny body pressed up tightly against his.

"You know," she says to him, snuggling up just a little bit closer, feeling his arm squeeze around her. "I have had many of the same thoughts lately. This is such a gorgeous place, I could totally see spending my whole life here, and I could certainly see spending the rest of it with you. It's nice to know that we've been thinking about the same things, and that we're on the same page."

Adam leans down and kisses the top of her forehead while she talks, inhaling the scent of her mixed with sunscreen and cheap hotel shampoo, feeling his heart swell with happiness. "I have traveled out this way a few times in my life, but I've never really been here on my own with someone special, and seen this place with adult eyes, had a chance to take in all the beauty and the life surrounding me. Thank you for coming here with me. This place is breathtaking. This is absolutely somewhere I would want to settle down and call home, and I want to do that with you Adam."

She squeezes his hand while she says this last part, and Adam can't help but lean down and pull her right up into his lap, beginning to kiss her deeply, wrapping his arms around her tightly. He couldn't be more happier or more in love with her in this moment if he tried.

This conversation has put them both at an ease they haven't felt with each other in a long time, with everything out in the open between them, and being able to relax and stretch their legs and just enjoy each other in normal life and time.

The rest of the afternoon passes in a happy blur together, with both of them lost on the high of each other and being here on vacation and in love. They're acting like teenagers who can't keep their hands off one another, everything feeling new and fresh, with so much excitement between them. They have everything they want here in this moment, with no thoughts of their past adventures, or what Adam has planned up his sleeve, to cross their minds and interrupt their good feelings.

Chapter Eleven

After having had such a wonderful day relaxing together and loving life right now, the pair decide to continue on into their evening the exact same way, acting like they are already settled and living the life of their dreams. No stress, no worries, no cares. They shower once more, washing the hot sun and ocean off their salty bodies and get dolled up to the nines before heading out to another fancy restaurant to enjoy a nice meal together.

They arrive at a lavish looking place, and as Adam holds the massive doors open for her to enter first, Demi laughs and makes a remark about how she could get used to living a life just like this, so fancy and free. Adam laughs with her and pulls her in close and kisses her forehead lightly. "You better get used to it baby, because this is all I ever want for us." He says huskily in her ear.

He sees an opening in this bit of conversation though. As they sit down at their table and get settled and order drinks, their conversation progresses and he steers them towards the idea of another robbery, because, as he says to her, "If they want to live every day like this, doing as they please and living comfortably, they may need to commit at least one more big crime, and one that's worth it, to make sure they're settled for life."

This little tidbit that Adam drops into the conversation does not go over quite the way he had thought it would when he had seen the opportunity and played this out in his head. He just assumed that she would take it as a joke and laugh it off or maybe even agree with him that they could use a little more gold coin lining their pockets if they want to continue living the life of luxury. He figured it would either open her up to the idea of it, or at least find some humor in it, especially after everything that they've been through.

Instead, it seems to spark something else in her entirely, and she shuts down slowly, and quietly, lost in the thoughts in her own head, unwilling to share what she's thinking with him. And because of this, their conversation dies, and Adam finds his own thoughts spiraling off.

At the mention of another crime again, he finds himself thinking about this upcoming robbery once more, and Brandon and his involvement with him, and he starts growing anxious and nervous and guilty as hell all over again, and just wants to get this over with and off his chest. He can't wait to tell Demi about everything he has planned and what he's been up to behind her back, and get it all out in the open.

He is still filled with guilt about hiding this from her, and he's also still a little torn about how she's going to feel about committing another crime, and the whole Brandon thing, but he assures himself once more that if he can find the right time to talk to her about it, when the mood is perfect and he's really thought over what he wants to say so he makes no mistakes, and he can get her to see the reasons why, she will give. She has to, because his reasoning behind it is perfect. He just wants to give them the absolute best life possible.

Once Demi has had a chance to digest everything and sees how easy this robbery is going to be with the help of Brandon, how it would be so much easier than the last heist they were involved in, of course she will say yes. Once she knows this time, there would be no reason for Demi to get too involved or get her hands dirty, pun intended, she was going to be just as excited as he was about it. It was just all about the timing in when to talk to her about it, and suddenly he found he was smiling to himself, thinking that planning this robbery seem to be just as tedious as finding the right time to ask her to marry him.

Demi catches Adam smiling to himself as they sit across from each other and eat dinner, but his smile bothers her, and she finds herself simply pushing the food around on her plate, unable to eat much, not finding she has much of an appetite anymore, her good mood faded.

She can't help where her train of thoughts have been going, and she finds that she's thinking back over their time together, back over the heist, and the kidnapping, and all of the crazy and wild things they've experienced together, things that weren't normal and so far from the life that she had envisioned for herself once upon a time.

All that she had wanted from this vacation and this time away from everything was a chance for them to really shut down from the world and be together, in the moment, and maybe figure out what a normal life together really was. She had envisioned them relaxing on the beach, soaking up the sun, eating good food and drinking and laughing, finally not having to be behind the wheel, driving from place to place and crime to crime, always on the go and on the run. Taking the time to explore one another all over again, enjoy some kinky sex, test each other's limits.

She had really wanted them to start thinking about themselves as a couple, and what they were going to do next, and what they were going to do with their future. Their real future, and their real life, because when you broke it right down, this was not much of a real life at all. This was just reckless Bonnie and Clyde shit, and she was tired of it.

But she can tell that his mind keeps wandering elsewhere, and she no longer thinks that it's just because they haven't had enough time yet to shut down and unwind and let go of everything that they've been through. Even though she has asked him a few times now, on a few different occasions, what's on his mind and what he's thinking about, he always tells her the same things; stress, traveling, crime, and that he needed this as much as she did. She's no longer so sure though, and she hates that she's starting to doubt him, and herself. There has got to be something behind that smile, and the way he keeps acting, so withdrawn and somewhat secretive.

They finish the rest of their dinner now mostly in silence, picking at their food while the crowded restaurant carries on around them; people chatting quietly, laughing, dishes rattling and glasses clanking. They may as well be lost inside their own little worlds, separate even from each other, both thinking thoughts they aren't sharing with the other. And both of them are thinking things that are worlds apart from the other.

    The mood has changed between them as well, and while it isn't quite heavy yet, or bad, it has brought down some of the happiness and the excitement that they had started the evening with. And while Demi picks up on it clearly, especially considering the way her own mood and thoughts have changed, Adam is far too in his own head to notice much of anything other than that Demi seems quieter than when they first came out to eat. He's still too focused on the plans and the future he's thinking about.

    Once they've finally finished dinner and paid the bill, they leave the restaurant but don't head back to the hotel right away; instead they hold hands and take a walk through the city, looking at the lights. Demi had hoped that a walk might break the mood up a bit and help shake the evening up, but Adam is still preoccupied, and what little conversation they were having dies.

    The silence between them starts to bother Demi though, all the questions and tidbits she tries to say simply blowing away unheard in the wind, and after the cold starts to break through to her too, she suggests that they cut their walk short and head back to the hotel. She's ready to just get back to their room and relax for a little while and go to sleep. Her head hurts, and she's feeling moody and tired.

    And not just tired in a sleepy sense, but she's tired of him only making small talk with her, too preoccupied with whatever is going on in his head, and she no longer believes him when he tells her that it's just stress and needing some time to relax. At this point, she just wants to call it a night and try to distract herself from all of this. She is convinced that he's lying to her about something, but she's frustrated with trying to break through to him, and done trying to figure out what's really going on here.

    There is something in her voice, or maybe it's the way that she's talking, but it's enough to get through to Adam and it snaps him out of his train of thoughts; going back and forth between this upcoming robbery, how it will affect their relationship, and proposing to Demi is tearing him up inside. And he realizes that something is off, and it could very well be because he's so caught up in his head, and hasn't given her the time and attention that he was supposed to tonight; the time and attention that she deserves.

He doesn't want to bring up the fact that things seem off right now, he doesn't want to mention anything to her in regards to that at all for fear of bringing up his comment about committing another crime again and opening up a doorway to a conversation that he isn't ready to have with her yet, but he knows he needs to stop and bring himself back to the present, right now. That's what they were supposed to be here doing together in the first place, and he doesn't want this mood that he's in affecting them anymore than it may already have.

Before they make it back to the hotel, Adam stops them right where they are walking, right in the middle of the sidewalk while people carry on around them, and he holds her close, kissing her passionately, completely taking her breath away. He holds her and kisses her like they're the only people in the world, like a scene out of the end of a romance movie.

He knows just how to touch her, how to kiss her, and what places she loves the most even without really getting too handsy with her in public or making a scene. Adam just knows her so well by now, inside and out, that he knows how to get her going and change her mood whenever he wants to.

When he finally does pull away from her and break their unexpected kiss, she is more than breathless; she's speechless. Her mind is blank and her worries are long gone, and she's got a smile on her face, her eyes half closed. That tender moment and being in his embrace was exactly what she needed to pull her out of the thoughts of turmoil rolling around in her brain.

Adam kisses her on the forehead, wrapping his arm around her and holding her close, feeling a sense of ease fall over them again, and happiness fills his stomach where doubt was only a few moments before. He tells himself that everything is going to work out perfectly, and they continue their walk once more, making their way back to their hotel room for the evening, holding each other tightly as they go.

Chapter Twelve

By the time they've made their way back into the hotel, up the elevator and to their room, everything has changed. Demi and Adam are holding hands and talking easily again, and the mood has shifted between them once more, back to a happier, more lighter feeling, with the stress of their dinner long behind them now.

Once they've unlocked the door and gone inside, Adam instantly orders her into the bathroom and starts running a bubble bath for her, before she can start stripping and getting ready for bed. He knows her too well by now. "I know you may be tired, but the night isn't over yet, my love. I would like for you to relax and take a little bit of time for yourself. Have a nice hot soak and put your mind at ease babe." He finishes this off with a light kiss on her lips before leaving the bathroom.

As she removes her clothing and slowly steps into the warm bubbly tub, Adam returns to the bathroom and brings her in a cold glass of wine, and lays out a set of pjs and one of the cozy hotel house coats on the side chair to wait for her until she's done. He reminds her to enjoy herself one more time, and then he places a light kiss on the top of her forehead this time and walks out of the bathroom, shutting the door behind him to give her some privacy and peace.

By the time they had begun heading back to their hotel room, and he had seen her mood change all over again, Adam realized without a doubt now that he had been the cause for the way she was feeling. He desperately wants to change her mood and get her back to feeling good and at ease with them again, her happy normal overly loving self that she usually is, laughing and glad to be with him, sharing everything with him. He just wants to see her smile and know that everything is ok between them, and he's feeling slightly antsy with himself, just wanting to be able to put all of this behind them.

While he waits for her to finish, he gets himself a

beer from the mini fridge and takes his phone out of his pocket. He scans it quickly, sees a couple of messages from Brandon, and he clears them, a wave of guilt washing over him once more. He turns his phone off and tosses it on his nightstand, and then heads out onto the balcony, wanting to get some fresh air into his lungs and have a chance to sit and settle his own mind, and the thoughts that are racing around in there.

He finds himself playing the scene from the restaurant over and over again in his head, dissecting their conversation and trying to pin point exactly what had set her off, now that he feels in his heart that it's him, and not something else she's going through. He worries he may have said something he shouldn't have, or something that set her off, and the more he dwells on it, the more he thinks that it was his offhand comment about needing to commit another crime that set her off. That seemed to be what started the decline of their wonderful evening out together.

The thought causes a pit of dread to form in his stomach, and he takes a deep breath and forces himself to push it aside. If that's the case, he thinks, than he must not have approached it right, that's all, and when he is ready to talk to her about what he's planning with Brandon, he just needs to find the exact time, way, and place to bring it up to her in. He's realizing more and more that this is going to be a touchy, delicate situation, especially considering their past and the way he's going about things right now, and he decides to put it off for a little while longer, until he's really had a chance to sit down and talk to Brandon and form a more solid plan about what they're going to do, and what he's going to say to Demi.

The anxiety of the build-up, the back and forth in his head, the what ifs and assumptions are all starting to drive him crazy, and now that he's here in LA he needs to get settled and make a plan, so that he can feel more secure about all of this. Once he's done that, he's sure he'll be in a much better state of mind himself, and then he'll be able to sit down with her and actually get through to her.

He just needs her to see that this is something that they really, truly, actually need to do, and not something that he just wants them to do on a whim, or because he's greedy, or impulsive. It's an easy job, and it's a massively profitable one, one that would finally put an end to all the other odd jobs and risky crimes they'd been committing. Brandon is the mastermind behind it, and he's an amazing criminal, and smart at what he does. This would give them a real, proper chance at the life they want, where there are no limits and they can follow their dreams together wherever they may lead. All Adam wants to do is give her the world. They just need this one last job to do that.

Now that Adam has had a chance to go over this in his head a few times, and he's feeling a bit more sorted out with the plan he's come up with, Adam takes a big swig of his beer, and then follows this up with a deep breath, allowing himself to feel satisfied. He has a good hunch that everything is going to work out perfectly, just as he's hoping.

He stares out over the lights and the ocean in front of him, midnight black but covered in the reflection of all the beautiful city lights, the stars, and the moon. He listens to the crashing waves and the occasional chatter of people's conversations that float up to him on the wind. He finds himself day dreaming about their future once more, a happy future, allowing himself to think big; having kids with her, traveling the world with their little family, having new experiences each and every day, and how wonderful that would all feel like to him, to finally achieve everything he's ever dreamed of.

At the same time that Adam is sitting out on the balcony enjoying himself and his evening, relaxing and winding down, basking in the moment, Demi is still in her hot bubble bath. She's soaking in water up to her chest, she still has the glass of wine in her hand that Adam had brought in for her, and she has absolutely everything that she needs to be nice and relaxed herself right now, only she isn't.

Demi is finding it impossible to shut her mind off

tonight, and to allow herself unwind and be in the moment. Her feelings are jumping all over the map, she can't seem to stay out of her head for more than a moment at a time, and she is so overwhelmed and can't seem to calm herself down or to be able to get a handle on her emotions, everything from stress, anxiety, happiness, uncertainty, and nervousness to confusion and almost sadness running through her veins.

 She, too, finds herself replying the scene from dinner in her head, running their conversation through her mind over and over, hearing their words on repeat. But mostly, she's got herself stuck on Adam's comment, the same one he thought she may have been hung up on, although he couldn't have imagined the way that it's making her feel.

 Something is nagging at her inside, and she is terrified that he's up to something behind her back, that he's doing something that he isn't supposed to, something that he hasn't been honest with her about. She has no idea what it could be, but she can't help but wonder if it's something he isn't telling her about the previous heist, or if it's something else entirely. What could he be up to behind her back?

 The thought that there may be something going on that she can't trust him to talk to her about is killing her, because after everything that they have been through together, and with the way things started between them, trust is something that is already fragile, and yet so incredibly important to her. She hates to think that honesty isn't something that's front and center important in his life like it is in hers.

 Trust is something that they need to be rebuilding together and working on brick by brick, not tearing apart still little by little. She needs to know that she can trust him with her life, and when she asks him about things like this, and tries to communicate with him, and she can tell that he's lying and keeping something from her, she just doesn't know how to feel, and she's having a hard time trying to put it past her and enjoy the moment. Because she's not even sure what's really happening in the moment.

And then on top of all of that, there is a nagging voice calling out from the back of her mind that all of this is simply in her head, and that not only is she reading too much into how Adam is feeling, but she's assuming things and making herself crazy over something that likely isn't actually happening anyway. She is driving herself nuts going back and forth, wondering if she's right, or if maybe she's just doubting herself and her ability to believe that he truly loves her and wants to be with her. And if there is nothing wrong with him, than she doesn't want to keep nagging him and bugging him and driving him crazy too, when she has no cause for any of this in the first place. Feeling frustrated, she decides to keep what she's feeling to herself for now.

It's hard, but she forces herself to focus and to shift her train of thoughts from those of negativity spiraling out of control to ones that are happier for her. She starts by taking a couple of long, deep breaths, and a sip of her wine. Then she starts thinking about their visit to the beach earlier that day, and their time vacationing here so far. The Demi starts imagining what life would actually be like living here on the beach with him, spending every single day together in happy bliss.

That puts her mind at ease, and after a little while of day dreaming about owning big beach houses, taking fancy vacations, having a gorgeous beach wedding filled with lots of wonderful friends, dinners with loved ones and traveling all over the world with Adam, and maybe one day having kids together, she finally feels settled and content enough to pull the plug and get herself out of the tub.

She takes her time putting herself together again after the bath, making herself feel good with all of her favorite lotions and creams, wanting to put herself in the most relaxed state possible. By the time she comes out of the bathroom, she's given herself a bit of a pampering, with her hair put up in a towel to dry and the robe wrapped tightly around her. She's skipped the pajamas underneath though, wanting to feel sexy, and now she is refreshed and ready for another glass of wine and to snuggle up with Adam out on the balcony. She's ready to end this day on a happier note, much like the way that it started.

Chapter Thirteen

Demi wanders out onto the balcony and takes a seat beside Adam, setting her glass of wine down on the table and pulling the house coat closer around her against the breeze from the ocean. The evening air is crisp, not chilly enough to give her goosebumps, but chilly enough to cause her to sit close on the chair beside him to gather up some of his warmth.

Once she's settled, she reaches for her wine once more and takes a long sip, and as she does, Adam watches her from the corner of his eye, trying to judge her mood. She seems to be a lot more happier and relaxed now, and so he decides to make sure he keeps it that way, and to not bring up anything else about their dinner conversation, crime, or anything about their past for that matter at all. Right now he just wants to soak up a little quality time with her, and enjoy being happy with her right here, right now.

He reaches over and grabs her free hand, giving it a little squeeze, and she smiles at him. It's one of those big, to her eyes smiles that he loves, and the look she gives him makes his heart race. He lets go of her hand and then reaches over and grabs her whole chair, sliding it that much closer to him, so that the arms of the chairs are touching, and he can easily reach out and wrap his arm around her, pulling her close.

Slowly they begin to chat, opening up to one another about other things they've been thinking about, and what's crossed their mind over the day. Neither of them bring up anything touchy, they just talk about life in general, and slowly begin to feel totally at ease with one another once more, all their problems from dinner time fading away.

Demi mentions to him that she's really enjoyed their first day of vacation together, and that the time they'd spent at the beach earlier had been the best time she'd had with him in a long time. "It was so nice to wake up this morning with absolutely nothing on the agenda. No pressure, no driving, nowhere to be, and nothing to run from," she says, and Adam agrees with her, seeing an opening to say something related, but to steer the conversation away from anything that might trigger a crappy mood again.

"I want us to get a house together soon, so we can have a real solid place for you and I to live," he says to her, "Somewhere we can call home, where we can truly settle down and start a real life together." She smiles and nods at this, and at the same time Adam leans forward in his seat and plants a sweet, gentle kiss on her smiling lips, causing her to giggle slightly when he pulls away.

She takes another sip of wine, feeling a tingling stirring inside of her that has nothing to do with the alcohol that she's drinking, and everything to do with the way that he makes her feel. She licks her lips slowly, the taste of beer lingering there from his kiss mixing in with the wine.

He always brings up all sorts of emotions inside of her, and makes her body experience feelings she's never felt before him, raw passion, desire, love, excitement, horniness, lust and need. Feelings of longing, feelings of want, and feelings she doesn't even know how to explain yet.

Another part of her begins to respond to his little kiss too. He is looking at her in such a way that she feels a throbbing and a tingling begin to form between her legs at what she knows is bound to happen next.

Demi sets her wine glass back down on the table, and the moment both of her hands are free, Adam is on her, scooping her up in his arms and pulling her over onto his own lap. At this point, he's also filled with excitement, anticipation, and he's eager to take her and have his way with her, filling her with his cock that's throbbing and aching in his pants for her, wanting to make her cum all over it, wanting to hear her moan his name.

Adam pulls her in close and Demi snuggles up comfortably in his lap, always loving the way that she seems to fit so nicely there. She's also loving the erotic contrast of being dressed only in her hotel housecoat, naked underneath, sitting on his lap while he's still fully dressed.

Then he's touching her, distracting her from her thoughts. He cups her face in his hands, his fingers warm on her cheeks. He pulls her face gently and turns her to look at him, pressing his lips to hers once more, kissing her gently and softly over and over. He covers her lips in little kisses as he feels her body start to soften and yield to him.

She moans gently under her breath, loving the feeling of his lips on hers, and when she does her lips part a little bit and his tongue slips through, softly caressing hers, and her moan grows louder at the unexpected intrusion. She grows more eager, and starts to thrust her hips into him and she wiggles her bum around on his lap while they make out on the balcony overlooking the ocean and the city lights.

Demi lets out a little shudder, but it isn't from the chilly night air, even though more wind caresses her body as Adam pulls her house coat open, exposing her. He keeps kissing her the entire time, never stopping as he slides his hand along her bare chest until he makes his way to one of her breasts, and slowly starts to pinch and pull at her nipple.

She lets out another moan, her body instantly responding to his touch, and her nipple stiffens and hardens under his exploring fingertips. After a few tweaks, rolling it between his fingers, pinching it and pulling on it, she feels his hand lightly caress over her skin and make its way over to her other one, finding that nipple already hard and waiting for him. He can't help himself, now it's his turn to moan into her mouth, loving how eager she is for him all the time, never saying no.

As he moans, she lets out a little smile against his lips, enjoying how she can turn him on simply with her body, and then, remembering something, she leans her face closer to the side of his and whispers quietly near his ear. "Mmm, this is just like that night we shared at another hotel, only a few short months ago, where you fucked me right out in the open on the balcony, taking me for the whole world to see."

Adam's moan turns into a growl at this, sounding like an animal. He pinches her nipple a little harder when she says this, getting a moan out of her too, remembering very clearly the night she's mentioning. It happened a few months back, just as Adam had brought up the idea of the jewelry heist to her. It had gone over terribly, and they had both gotten very mad at each other, gotten drunk and then fallen apart, getting into a fight at the hotel. From there, they had shared amazing make up sex, fucking like horny teenagers while they stared out over the city skylights.

Adam feels his cock twitch in his jeans, and he takes her by the hips and slightly shifts the way that she's sitting on his lap, so that he can feel her grinding against him even more. Then he starts to kiss down her neck and along her collar bone, while still touching and gently tugging on her nipples at the same time. Her house coat begins to fall to the side, sliding almost right off of her now and totally exposing her body to the chilly air. "I think that's a night I'd like to recreate with you, minus all the drinking and fighting, right here and now."

Demi can feel her body react to this before her mind has a chance to connect to her mouth, and so instead of replying all she can really do is moan, leaning back a bit and thrusting her body forwards, presenting herself to him, allowing him to use her as he will. He eagerly pulls her housecoat the rest of the way off of her, letting it fall onto her lap, and he moves his mouth lower, kissing and nibbling and licking his way to her chest.

He makes his way down further, now cupping one of her soft breasts in his hand and raising it up just enough that he can place her nipple to his mouth, lightly rubbing his wet lips over it. Then he blows on it softly and she lets out a cry at his teasing, shifting her ass in his lap again, thrusting herself into him, eager for more.

Adam can now feel his cock straining in his boxers,

rock hard and pressing up against her leg, eager for release. He can't wait until just a little while longer, when he can free it and slide it up against the wetness that he can feel is growing between her own legs, as her dampness causes a heat on his thigh while she sits and wiggles her naked self on top of him.

He's desperate to feel that dampness somewhere else though, especially if he's not quite ready to fuck her yet, and so while his mouth keeps busy at her chest level, licking and sucking and nibbling on her little nubs, his hand makes its way lower, and he feels her legs part eagerly for him and his hand finds itself nestled between her bare naked legs.

Adam ever so gently and slowly runs his fingertips along the length of her slit, just lightly caressing her, and her whole body shudders and reacts to his touch. She is already soaking wet, and he can feel just the hint of her dampness along the crease of where her lips part as she spreads her legs wider, opening herself up for him, wanting him. At the same time she lets out a little panting moan, tossing her head backwards, breathing heavy.

Just as his tongue teases and tastes her nipples, his fingers begin to do the same to her hot mound. He applies just enough pressure that she can feel his fingers there, spreading her wetness around, opening her up, but not touching her how she wants. Her body cries out as she does, demanding more and more as she shifts and moans in his lap, Adam never giving in and only touching her enough to tease her.

"You are making me crazy baby, please, stop driving me wild and take me already, I need to cum for you!" Demi begs as she shakes again, her pussy soaking now and throbbing for him, wanting so badly for him to take her, to devour her and make her cum again and again.

Adam doesn't answer her at first, he doesn't do anything else other than to keep teasing her for just a few more minutes, and then right when she is about ready to burst and start begging and pleading with him some more, he reaches up and grabs her robe and pulls it away entirely from where it's been piled on her lap like a blanket, leaving her sitting there completely naked on his lap. She is totally exposed now, at his mercy and on display in the dark evening light, surrounded by the ocean, the city lights and all the other balconies around them.

He takes her all in in the dim glow, looking at her up and down slowly, loving the sight of her there, and the look on his face causes Demi to bite her bottom lip in anticipation of what's to come next. Then he says to her in a gruff voice, "Stand up, and walk over to the ledge, looking out over the ocean." The authority in his voice doesn't give her much room to argue with, not that she would have anyway. She absolutely loves it when he dominates her and takes control of her like this, knowing that she can let go and trust him completely. He knows her body so well, he knows *her* so well; her wants, desires, needs, beliefs, even her limits, and when to push them to new places, and when to stop. She loves the feelings he creates in her, and constantly has her craving for more and more.

So she doesn't even hesitate, she stands up and confidently gives him a little show as she does so, turning herself around slowly and giving her ass a little shake towards him. Then she saunters over to the balcony ledge, which stands about chest level with her, and she places her arms on the upper portion and bends a little bit, putting herself on display for him, knowing he is watching her closely.

Her breasts are pressed up tightly against the rough concrete wall, and her body shivers again, both from the chill of the night that she's feeling and all the excitement and anticipation that's building up inside of her for what's to come next. She looks out at the view before her, inhaling a deep breath of salty ocean air, taking everything in all around her, absolutely loving everything about her life in this moment, where she is, who she's become, and the fact that she's about to be taken by the man that she loves.

Adam doesn't rush either, biding his time, waiting a moment and staying seated on the chair behind Demi, taking in the view of a different kind in front of him. She is gorgeous, and her body is a silhouette in the dark shadows here, the city lights and the ocean stretched out before her. He loves her plump little perky round ass, and her tiny waist, and her long hair that cascades down to meet them. Her body is perfect, soft and smooth and waiting for him, his hands, mouth, his cock. She is all his.

    He stands up and slowly, without taking his eyes off of her form, begins to strip himself of his own clothes right there on the balcony beside her discarded robe, leaving them standing there both in the nude. Demi never turns around during this either, instead she simply closes her eyes and focuses on the sound of his clothing being removed and hitting the floor. His belt buckle clangs on the floor, echoing slightly around the balcony and it only adds to her level of excitement, knowing that pleasure is not too far off now.

    Walking up behind her, Adam ever so slowly reaches out and runs his hands down her back, gently, teasingly, feeling the softness of her skin in contrast against the roughness of his palms. He never keeps his hands in one place long, just touching her everywhere, lightly with his fingertips and then a little firmer with his whole hand, and then back to his fingertips. He runs his hands along her sides, her stomach, her thighs, no where she wants to feel them yet still loving the feeling of having them everywhere, teasing her and driving her mad all at once. He can feel her entire body shaking, trembling, vibrating under his hands as she breaks out into goosebumps under his touch.

    Demi moans loudly now, unable to help herself against the sounds that she's making. Her eyes are closed, her hips are swaying back against him, and her entire being feels like it's on fire for him, begging for him physically. Her pussy is throbbing, and she's so wet that she can feel it starting to drip down her leg, causing her thighs to grow slippery while they rub and press together as she grinds against him. She thrusts her hips backwards harder, begging him now to fuck her, to take her, to fill her aching hole. "Please, Adam I need you," she moans under her breath, as she moves and shifts her body and her nipples rub into the rough wall in front of her, turning her on even more.

Adam reaches down and takes the base of his thick veiny cock in his hand, his grip firm, and he slowly strokes himself a few times. He debates just leaning forward and ploughing into her, filling her like she's begging to be filled, feeling her wet hole engulf him, but he decides to wait just a little bit longer, and see if he can't tease her and drive her just a little more wild, even though it's driving him crazy as well, pre-cum oozing from the tip of his cock.

He does lean forward, but instead of sliding his cock into her aching vagina, he reaches around her with his free hand and slides it between her spread open legs. He cups her hot mound with his whole hand, holding her, feeling just how wet and ready she really is for him.

Then he uses his fingers to apply a little bit of pressure, wiggling them along her lips, and then he spreads his fingers wide, parting her pussy lips with them, exposing her moist, intimate area. Finally, he does lean forward a little more, and with his other hand holding himself steady, he ever so gently rubs the head of his cock against her folds, feeling her jump at his touch and moan as the silky head slides up and down her wet slit, covering himself in her juices.

This is torture in itself for both of them, and as she begs and moans and tries to throw her hips backwards, forcing herself on him, he holds her steady, his hand that had been cupping her is now on her hip, continuing to keep her still, taking his time and getting himself lubed up, getting them both primed and ready and as horny as possible for one another.

When even he can take the teasing no longer, when he feels like he's almost ready to explode under the pressure, and he knows she's only moments away from an orgasm herself, he finally lets go of his cock and slams forward into her. He fills her completely, ramming all the way into her hard in one thrust, causing them to both cry out into the night.

Having been teased so badly by Adam for so long, Demi is beside herself with lust and need. She's so horny and wet she can feel her juices leaking out of her already, covering him and dripping down her thighs, making the sound of his cock slamming in and out of her so wet and sloppy, turning her on more and more.

Demi reaches up and grips onto the ledge in front of her for leverage, holding on tightly, her nails digging in and pushing herself backwards to meet him thrust for thrust as he takes her from behind, pounding her harder and harder. His cock feels so good inside of her, stretching her, fucking her, hitting all the good spots as it slides almost all the way out of her, the head stretching her open wide, before slamming back in again.

Adam can tell that it won't be long before she cums all over him, her tight silky walls are squeezing his penis tighter and tighter every time he pulls his cock out of her, ready to slide it back in again and again. She is so wet and slippery, and he can feel his balls smacking into her lips and brushing her clit every time he moves forwards again, making her cry out.

He starts dirty talking to her, leaning forward and whispering in her ear that he loves how tight she is, that he loves taking her sweet little pussy, that she feels so good squeezing and milking his cock. He tells her how wet she is, and how he loves feeling her juices drip down out of her, coating his cock and covering their legs. "I love that I can turn you on so much, making you soaking wet for me."

Then he reaches down around her once more, cupping her mound and holding her close, letting his fingers make their way around her wet folds until he comes into contact with her hard little clit. He ever so gently and slowly starts rubbing circles around it, pressing down on the hood, making her moan louder and buck and thrash her body backwards against him, wanting more, desperate to cum. In doing so she forces his cock to push that much further inside of her, brushing her cervix, and she shudders, so close to orgasm.

Adam knows that he's pushed her as near to an orgasm as she's going to get before she cums, and so he leans in that much closer, his mouth pressed right against her ear, his breath warm. "Are you going to cum for me baby?" He whispers roughly, then licks and nibbles along her ear lobe, breathing lightly on it as she shivers. He keeps touching all her sensitive spots, turning her on immensely and forcing her to give into her orgasm that's flowing though her.

Demi's entire body is tingling, from her fingertips to her toes, and she starts to shudder and vibrate against him as a low moan escapes the back of her throat, sounding almost primal. She throws herself backwards against him, using the ledge to push herself, her hips slamming backwards into him, forcing his cock to bottom out inside of her as she begins to cum, squeezing and tightening around him.

He holds her hot, sweaty, shaky body close to him while she cums, although he never lets up fucking her, his hips pounding into her ass repeatedly as his cock slides in and out of her, bringing him closer to cumming with every thrust as well. The tightness and silky wetness of her tunnel is just too much for him, now that it's clamping shut around his cock and almost seeming to suck in him deeper, keeping him in there, squeezing around him like a vise while she cums.

Even though he is close to cumming himself, Adam holds off, but keeps up the pace for a few more minutes as she cums. But as soon as he feels her orgasm begin to subside, as her body grows still in his arms and her pussy stops spasming, he is quick to switch things up, wanting his turn for release. Demi feels his hard cock slide out from her slippery, still slightly twitching hole, and then in that voice she loves, she hears him tell her, "Turn around and get on your knees."

Once more Demi does as she's told, eager to please him now as he's pleased her, and she spins herself around, dropping out of sight on the balcony, getting down on the cold concrete on her knees. She gets settled then looks up at him with her big bedroom eyes, giving him a smile and then opening her mouth wide towards him and inviting him to take her exactly as he pleases.

    Adam stokes his cock once slowly, looking down at her, and now it's his turn to bite his bottom lip as he lets out a little sigh. "Mmm," he moans softly, "I love you, and that pretty little mouth of yours," before he reaches down and lightly grabs her around the face and throat, moving forward and thrusting his cock into her open, waiting mouth.

    He slips in past her wet lips and starts to face fuck her slowly, gently, sliding his cock in and out of her mouth, opening her up and pushing his cock in further and further back into her throat, feeling her gag slightly when he goes in a little too far. Demi can taste her own juices on him, mixing with the pre-cum from the head of his cock, and the taste turns her on. She eagerly runs her tongue around his hard member in circles, and then up and down the shaft, licking up every last drop.

    She raises one of her hands to his cock and wraps her soft tiny fist around the base of it, giving it a tight squeeze. Then she slowly starts to stroke him, up and down the length of him, keeping pace with the movement of his cock in her mouth. Sometimes she moves her fist around in circles, and sometimes she just strokes him harder and faster.

    The sound of her sucking and slurping on his cock, and the occasional sound she makes when she gags on it, feeling her throat tighten and constrict around the head of his cock is driving him wild, never mind the feelings of her lips, tongue and mouth mixed in with her expert hand. He knows he isn't going to last much longer before he blows his load in her sweet mouth.

    He picks up his speed, his hands on the back of her head now as she places her other hand on his thighs to give her a little bit of control. Adam glances up over the balcony and out into the ocean as he feels her lips tighten around his shaft again and her tongue caress the head of his cock, and then he feels his balls tighten and his stomach clench as she pushes him over the edge. He gives in to his orgasm and cums hard in her mouth, spraying the back of her throat with his thick, salty cum.

Demi swallows, and then softly licks his shaft clean before pulling away, but it takes a minute for Adam to catch his breath and get his bearings again, coming back down from that amazing high before he reaches down and helps her get to her feet. Then his legs give out once more, and they collapse back down into Adam's chair, this time both of them naked while she cuddles into his lap.

They stay that way for a few more minutes, breathing heavy and snuggling, letting their heart rates relax and bodies cool down before they make their way back inside their hotel room for the night.

Chapter Fourteen

They awake the next morning and start their day as they've started to grow accustomed to; being lazy, having coffee, and relaxing with nowhere to be and nothing to do, enjoying this new time in their life. Demi may love it, but as the day progresses, Adam finds himself starting to grow restless with anxiety at his upcoming plans, filled with a need to actually start doing something and putting things in motion.

Adam doesn't want to keep going on in this limbo much longer, hiding things from Demi until he knows more and feels comfortable talking to her. He's only had a chance to text Brandon a few of times, trying to do it on the sly when Demi isn't looking, and so Adam hasn't even finalized a meeting with him yet. He feels anxious and nervous and a little bit sick to his stomach.

He is desperate to just do this. He needs to take action and get everything that he's begun to pile on his plate out into the open. He's really feeling torn about everything, constantly second guessing himself and driving himself crazy, and Adam has finally decided that enough is enough, no more stalling. Especially because he's growing increasingly worried and can't shake this nagging feeling in the pit of his stomach that something could go wrong and spiral out of his control before he's ready to come clean.

He's been trying to keep his cool, wondering what his next plan of action should be, but he's starting to get snappy. Thankfully, just after lunch, he has an idea while they are lounging around the hotel room, making plans for the afternoon. He tells Demi to go out for the rest of the day, by herself, and spoil herself totally. "I want you to find a really nice spa, and check yourself in for the afternoon and get a massage and a facial," he says that last part with a chuckle, as he can never take that seriously, "and then go out and get your hair and nails done, or whatever it is you would like to do, and even go do some shopping if you want. I want you to go out and enjoy yourself and get your pampering on, and come back here later looking relaxed and refreshed."

The fact that Adam may have an ulterior motive to not want to spend the afternoon with her never even crosses Demi's mind. After the last few amazing days that they've had, except for the little conversation mishap that happened at dinner last night, she's been relaxed and joyous and carefree, and has totally fallen into the fancy vacation down time mode. A few hours at the spa, followed up by some pampering and shopping sounds amazing to her.

She does ask him what he plans to do with his free afternoon though, now that she will be gone until a late dinner or so, and he laughs awkwardly at being put on the spot, feeling nervous and trying to think quick, to cover up how he's feeling. Adam tells her that he plans to do a whole lot of sweet fuck all while she's away. "I am probably just going to nap, and then go drink some beer and nap by the pool. Maybe I'll swim a few laps, catch some sun, and drink a lot more beer after that, while I come back up here and watch some TV or something. That sounds like my idea of total guy relaxation for the day."

Demi lets out a laugh and turns to start getting ready, but Adam feels a twinge of guilt in his gut while he stares at her back, having to swallow past a lump of yuck that's formed in his throat at lying to her so easily like that. He doesn't say much while she changes her clothes and packs up her purse, fighting with his emotions, but he does manage to hide it long enough to give her a kiss on the forehead and to say that he loves her and to have a good time before she walks out of the hotel room, leaving for a fabulous spa and rich girl afternoon.

For her, from that moment on for the rest of that afternoon, Demi is feeling free, relaxed and happy, as if she is on top of the world. She couldn't be any happier with the way that their vacation is going and by how amazing things feel between them, open and happy and loving. Demi smiles to herself as she gets on the elevator, hoping she feels this way forever, and feeling excited to be heading out to the spa.

    The only thing that would have made that afternoon better for her would have been to have girlfriends to share it with, and she feels a little twinge of hurt at that thought. The one thing that's been a downer to their life on the road is that she's begun to lose touch with all of her friends from her old life, even the close ones, and she misses having someone other than Adam to share her life with. She finds herself thinking that she'll be able to make some new friends once they finally find a place and get settled with their life, and then she forces the thoughts aside, getting on with her awesome afternoon.

    Adam wants to grab his cell phone and call Brandon the moment Demi shuts the door behind her, but he forces himself to wait for a few minutes, puttering around, giving her time in case she forgot something and needed to come back, not wanting to look suspicious to her. Once he's sure that she's gone though, he's quick to grab his cell phone and tun it on, giving Brandon a call.

    The guys talk for a few minutes, then decide to grab a beer and some wings at a restaurant down the road from the hotel Adam and Demi are staying at, so it's walking distance for him. They don't meet at the hotel restaurant for obvious reasons, and Adam gets that sneaky, guilty feeling in his stomach again like he's cheating on Demi, doing things behind her back that he shouldn't be. He partially scolds himself and reminds himself one more time that he's just doing this to get a proper plan together, and then he's going to talk to her at the right moment later in time, the sooner the better, when he can explain everything the way he needs to, in the best way possible so that she'll understand and be on board.

    When the guys finally meet up and get seated at the restaurant, making sure to be seated at a secluded table with no close neighbors to eavesdrop, with some beer and wings in front of them, Adam finds it feels really good to just sit and relax and catch up together with another man. Adam hadn't really given much thought to the fact that he's with a woman 24/7, constantly on the go, but it's very different and slightly nostalgic to be spending time together with Brandon once again like this, and to just be shooting the shit with another guy in general.

It doesn't take long in their conversation as they catch up before Brandon is killing himself laughing and tickled fucking pink by absolutely everything that he's been hearing from Adam. From the fact that Adam's actually still with Demi, they're in love, and Adam even wants to marry her, to the heist that they were involved in, and Demi's part with the jeweler's wife, to the fact that it all started by an accidental gas and go, when the new couple had no reason to be stealing at all. And Brandon's both amazed and amused by the fact that Adam snuck out here this afternoon to hang out with Brandon, and that Demi has absolutely no idea what he's planning or what he's up to, or that he's even been talking to Brandon at all, never mind putting together the ideas for a robbery that involves her.

"So what does she really think you're getting up to this afternoon then?" Brandon asks him with another laugh, before taking a swig of his beer and shaking his head. "Oh, sitting around the hotel pool, snacking and getting drunk, or having a nap in the hotel room with the TV on. Either or are where I plan to be when she gets back." Adam replies, taking a long drink of his own beer, feeling that wave of guilt wash over him again and trying to drink it away.

He still feels an awful pit of dread form in his stomach whenever he thinks about confronting her with what he's been doing behind her back, but he tells himself that it's simply because he still doesn't have a proper plan of action yet, and once he knows how to approach this, everything will be fine. He thought that would have come to him by now, or especially once he'd had a chance to chat with Brandon, but he's sure he'll figure it out eventually.

Adam forces himself to refocus and think about the bigger picture here, and what he is actually doing this for. Once this is all done and over with, after Demi's gotten on board and the crime is committed, and they're settled, and set for the rest of their lives, set for a wonderful, incredible, no limits kind of life, they're going to be so happy, and even more in love when they're married. Then they'll finally be able to put all of this behind them forever, and that thought helps change his mood and his mind set. Adam pulls himself back into the here and now and his conversation with Brandon with a better focus.

  The guys talk for a little while longer, slowly hashing out plans and scenarios and things they'll have to go over as it gets closer to the robbery, and Demi is more involved and on board. The time passes quickly and easily, more so for Adam, who had been lacking this in his life. It doesn't even seem like that long before the waitress is eyeing them funny because they're still there long after their beer and wings are done, but then Adam's phone goes off with a text message from Demi. It shows off a picture of some new shoes that she'd bought, followed by another text letting him know that she'd be heading back to the hotel shortly. He has definitely been here more than a few hours, no matter how fast the time had seemed to fly.

  They pay their tabs and then the guys part ways, making plans to chat again tomorrow. After, Adam heads back to the hotel, his thoughts spinning around wildly out of control in his head. He finds himself thinking about everything, from the conversation he'd just had with Brandon and the future robbery, right back to the very first moment he'd seen Demi sleeping in her bed before he kidnapped her that night with Brandon. And then for the first time in a little while, he reaches into his pocket and plays with the ring he's still got tucked inside, thinking about their future together.

  Adam hasn't asked her to marry him yet, and he's still so torn on doing so, or how. He wants it to be perfect, and memorable, and unique, something that she will love, but he doesn't want it to feel forced or fake either. And he also doesn't want all of this crime and guilt he's harboring inside caught up in the middle of it. He convinced himself once more that the right time to propose will be after he's opened up to her about what he's planning behind her back. This indecision is driving him absolutely crazy though. What has he done to himself?

Chapter Fifteen

Adam rushes back to the hotel, his thoughts still racing and his heart hammering loudly in his chest. He feels sweat break out and roll down his back as he anxiously boards the elevator, the wait for it feeling more like forever instead of about 3 minutes. He almost runs down the hallway to their room, quickly changing into his swim suit and then grabbing himself a beer and a towel. He has about five minutes to spare by the time he manages to get himself down to the pool in the late evening sunshine.

Since the moment that she had text him about heading back, he had felt absolutely sick to his stomach with worry and anxiousness, a pit of guilt so big forming in his stomach that he can't even stomach taking a sip of beer. He was terrified that she was going to come back early, and even though he's sure a simple "I went for a walk" would have been sufficient enough to cover up why he wasn't at the hotel like he said he was, he doesn't want to have to lie to her any more than he already has, or has to still. He feels like this is all starting to spiral faster than he's prepared for.

His emotions and feelings keep flipping all around inside of him, out of his control, confusing him. He keeps going back and forth between whether this is all a good decision or a bad decision, and it's eating him up inside. He regrets never having opened up to her about this in the first place. He truly had no idea how much guilt and torture he was going to feel inside about going behind her back like this and keeping something from Demi, even if he feels like his intentions are good, most of the time.

But only a few moments later, Adam glances up to see Demi saunter out of the hotel doors, heading towards the pool area, looking straight at him, and all his thoughts of turmoil and uncertainty are suddenly gone. Vanished, just like that. She is wearing a gorgeous brand new bathing suit, with a pretty flowered sarong wrapped around it, and pretty strappy sandals to match. Her hair has been freshly done and her face and skin are just glowing with happiness.

Demi looks like a million bucks, like she doesn't have a care in the world, and that is certainly the way that she feels inside right now. It radiates off of her from the inside out. Every single head turns to stare at her as she walks by, and Adam feels his own jaw drop in amazement at how damn good she looks. Something else inside of him stirs as she walked towards him as well. She just looks so damn sexy, he can't help himself.

As she draws closer, she makes eye contact and smiles at him, and a thought flies through Adams head, "She's the one. She loves me, I can see it in her eyes. I know it, and she's the woman I'm going to spend the rest of my life with. There is no doubt about that. She's going to say yes. To everything."

Demi is still grinning from ear to ear by the time she reaches Adam's chair, filled with incredible happiness, but that grin turns into a full on squeal when Adam jumps to his feet, grabbing her and picking up her into his arms, squeezing her tightly. People around them are still staring, and some are smiling and laughing with them, but they're oblivious to anything but one another.

She laughs and hugs him back, feeling the love between them flowing happily and freely. "Now, will you put me down please, people are staring at us," she says, finally feeling the eyes and growing a tad embarrassed, but still unable to stop giggling, feeling like she's high. He finally does let her drop to her feet, although reluctantly, and then he tells her that he just couldn't help himself with her looking so yummy and delicious like she is.

It's just past a regular dinner time, but the sun is still scorching hot and it feels good to relax together, so the pair decide to stay by the pool a little while longer and soak up a bit more sun before they finally grow tired and a bit hungry and restless and make their way back into the hotel and up to their hotel room.

Demi needs to get out of her swim suit and get

changed, and as she does, Adam can't help but stop what he's doing and simply stand there and stare, so enthralled by her and the way she looks. There is something about her, the new clothes that she's put on, the way her hair is done, the way she's glowing and just looks so happy and relaxed and beautiful, that stops his heart and catches his breath in his throat.

It's in that moment that Adam truly throws everything that he's feeling and harboring out the window for now. He admits to himself that every time he's tried to give her the evening and the vacation that she's so desperately been wanting from him, he's found a way to screw it up somehow, bring up things he shouldn't, or getting stuck inside of his head, bringing the mood down. Or, he adds to himself sourly, going around behind her back and getting himself feeling all sorts of miserable and guilty that it begins to rub off on her and their time together even when he's trying so desperately hard not to. She deserves to be treated, hell, they both deserve to be treated, exactly the way they keep talking about.

"Get something fancy on baby. Then grab your purse, because we're going out," he tells her while she's still changing, and when her eyes widen at him in curiosity, he simply shrugs at her mysteriously and tells her, "You'll see. But you look far too good for us to be staying in tonight."

They leave the hotel on foot and wander over a couple of streets until they find a nice place they haven't ate dinner at yet. They're holding hands periodically throughout the meal, talking easily, laughing together, and the evening flows smoothly with no mention of crimes, or their future, or anything that may cause pressure or strain on them this time. It's simply perfect.

Dinner seems to fly by, even though they are there for a few hours, and they both remark on how amazing the evening has been, how relaxed and carefree they both feel, how happy they are right now.

Afterwards, they leave the restaurant still holding hands and walk for a while until they've made their way down towards the beach, taking in the lights of the city glowing brightly to one side of them, and the beautiful view of the ocean to the other. The moon is so bright tonight, and already high in the sky, reflecting a shimmering glow on the water, and the sound of the waves crashing against the surf all around them is soothing and hypnotic.

Demi lets out a sigh that feels like it comes from deep within her soul, her whole body relaxing with contentment, so happy to be here with him in this moment. She steps away slightly, letting go of his hand and walking closer towards the water, inhaling the salty ocean air into her lungs.

Adam finds himself simply standing there and staring at her, actually more like gawking at her, with the dumbest expression on his face, just taking her all in, and everything that surrounds her. She is so beautiful standing there with the ocean like a backdrop underneath the moonlight, with the biggest smile on her face, eyes closed, living in the moment.

It's right there and then that it hits him; this would be the most perfect, natural time to propose to her. But of course, as life would have it, this was the evening he had decided to throw all the stress and pressure of everything building up out the window, and truly just enjoy their time in the moment together, and so he'd left the ring back at the hotel, tucked safely into a tiny pocket in another pair of jeans.

He chuckles softly to himself, the sound too low to be heard with her back to him, facing the steady crashing of the waves. Everything happens for a reason, he thinks to himself, especially since he hadn't had a chance to talk to her about the crime he was planning with Brandon, it was probably for the best that he didn't ask her tonight.

But hell, he thinks, if she doesn't look so beautiful standing there under the moonlight, the beach dark around them, so quiet, bright lights to one side, moonlight overhead. He tucks the vison away in his memory, thinking that it's perfect anyway, and then he takes a few

steps over towards her and grabs her hand, smiling at her.
  They resume walking down the beach, taking in the sights all around them, and talking quietly for a while before changing direction and heading back towards their hotel room for a little late night fun before bed.

Chapter Sixteen

As Demi slides her key into the hotel door, Adam steps right up behind her, his warm body pressed tightly against hers, running his hands up and down her exposed arms, making her shiver. As her hand reaches for the doorknob, he's leaning down and kissing along her neck and shoulders lightly, and her body breaks out into goosebumps.

She's barely got the door open and he's shoving against her, eager for them both to be inside, and alone. Once they're passed that threshold, he's quick to slam the door shut behind them, blocking them out from the rest of the world.

Adam doesn't know what's come over him, but he needs her, badly, more than he's ever needed her before. He isn't sure if it was all the romance tonight, the intense feelings of love, that missed opportunity to propose to her on the beach or what, but whatever it is, he is throbbing in his jeans, hard as a rock and ready to bend her over and have his way with her something terrible. Although he has other plans first.

Demi turns to face him, and he grabs her chin lightly in his hands, pressing his face down to hers and kissing her lips lightly, tenderly, little butterfly kisses almost before he pulls away from her. "I love you, Demi," he says, looking in her eyes, his hands now on her arms. "I love you too, Adam, you're the best thing that's ever happened to me," she replies, wrapping her arms around his waist and pulling herself close to him.

They stand like this for a minute, holding one another, but Demi can feel something hard poking into her from the front of his pants, and she doesn't think it's his belt buckle. As for herself, she can feel a growing wetness of her own between her legs, eager for a little late night fun herself.

Slowly, she grinds her hips into him, just a little sway at first before beginning to press harder into him, and Adam responds by moving his hands from her arms to her hips, pulling her right into him eagerly, and now she can definitely feel his hard cock poking into her. Adam looks down at her with a smile, and winks at her, and Demi lets out a giggle, then bites her bottom lip when he asks her if she's ready for him.

Adam leans down and kisses her once more, then moves his body forward, causing her to take a step backwards, pushing them towards the bed. She complies happily, stepping in time with him while still locked in each other's embrace. This continues until her knees hit the back of the bed, and then they buckle out from under her, and Adam lets her go, allowing her to fall backwards onto the bed in front of him.

Demi stares up at him, watching him watch her, and then she reaches down and grabs the hem of her dress and hikes it up a notch. Slowly, she starts exposing her long tanned legs, and now it's his turn to bite his lower lip. She loves how much she can turn him on, she loves how much he loves her body.

Adam lets her have her fun for a little bit, but the moment he sees a hint of her panties peek through he loses it. He jumps on the bed between her spread open legs, causing her to let out a giggling squeal, and then he grabs her around her hips and shifts her forwards on the bed so that he's got a little bit more room to lay down between her legs. Demi helps shift herself the rest of the way, and then she lays back down on the bed, relaxing, knowing exactly what he wants.

He gets comfortable between her legs, sliding her dress the rest of the way up. Her tanned thighs are spread before him, and her tiny red panties barely cover her mound. There's a damp patch on the middle of them, and he leans forward and blows on it ever so lightly, teasing her, watching her hips thrust upwards for more, listening to her sigh and moan. Adam does this one more time, but this time he reaches up and lightly runs the tip of one of his fingers down the length of her covered slit.

This sets her right off, desperate for him, and she

practically shoves her hips up into his face, reaching down to grab onto the top of his head. "Oh, fuck Adam, please don't tease me like this," she says with a moan, thrashing around on the bed. She can already tell that she's soaked and her pussy is throbbing, begging to be uncovered and tasted.

Adam just laughs softly at first, and then rubs his finger up and down the length of her again, with just a little bit more pressure this time, feeling her warmth and wetness soaking through the thin material. She moans once more, and then he leans forward and presses his mouth to her warmth, almost cupping her, breathing on her and running his tongue along her panties, tasting her right through them.

Demi lets out a cry, throwing her thighs up over his shoulders, grabbing at his hair now, desperate for more. Adam reaches up with one hand and pulls her panties to the side, finally exposing her, but just breaths on her wet folds, not licking her like she wants. "Adam!!" Demi all but screams his name, begging him now, squeezing him with her thighs. She can feel her pussy throbbing, aching to be touched, licked, tasted, desperate to cum.

Adam snakes out his tongue as far as he can and gives her one long lick, right up the center of her, making her jump, stopping right at her clit. Then he pulls away, sneaking his body out from her tangled legs and getting up on his knees on the bed, and then he lets out a laugh. "If you want me that badly babe, you better lose these thongs, and fast."

He actually has to refrain from letting out another laugh as he watches her scramble in her dress on the bed to strip herself of her panties, adjusting her legs around him. He isn't sure if it's all the drinking they've done tonight, or just all the romance that they've shared, but she's clearly just as horny as he is tonight, and he is eager to please.

It doesn't take more than a moment before she's sprawled back out before him on the bed, legs spread to either side of him, still wearing her dress, but now it's hiked right up past her hips. She is naked from the waist down, and her vagina is on full display for him, glistening with juices and her lips slightly spread open already, as she shifts and wiggles her hips for him. "Are you coming in for a taste big boy." She says, shifting herself one more time as she lays back on the bed, her feet towards the edges of the mattress.

She looks fucking delicious, and Adam feels his cock twitch in response in his jeans. All in due time, he thinks to himself, before laying back down on the bed between her legs and getting comfortable once more.

Slowly, he reaches up with one hand and touches her lips gently with the tips of his fingertips, feeling them slide easily along her wetness. Then he spreads her, opening her wide as her hips shift in excitement and she moans once more. He wonders if she's going to cum before he's even had a chance to really please her. He places his mouth right next to her once more, inhaling her sweet scent, before running his tongue along her slit again. Once more he starts at the bottom and slides all the way up until he reaches her clit, but this time he doesn't stop.

Demi throws her head back into the bed as his lips surround her hard little nub, licking on it and sucking on it, pulling it into his mouth, driving her crazy. He lets it fall from his lips and then drags his tongue back down her folds to her tight little opening, pushing his way inside, tasting her juices as it pools out of her.

He feels her fingers digging into the back of his head, pulling him into her pussy, wanting more. He's happy to give her what she wants. He takes two fingers and gently guides them into her waiting hole, alongside of his tongue, lubing them up and wiggling them around inside of her. He keeps licking and probing at her hole with his tongue at the same time, and her thighs shift as she tries to open herself up even more to him, letting him have her.

Adam can feel her pussy contracting around him, squeezing his fingers, wetness dripping out of her. He moves his mouth upwards, sucking on her folds, her lips, pulling on them slightly while his fingers are still buried inside of her. He reaches her clit once more, feeling it hard and ready, poking out from under its hood. He sucks it into his mouth lightly, twirling his tongue around it in circles, hearing her cry out, her body shaking and tightening up underneath him.

He knows her first orgasm isn't going to be long now, but he's feeling naughty tonight, and wants to give her an extra special one. Slowly, he lets her clit fall from his mouth, and once again he drags his warm tongue through her wet folds, stopping briefly when he meets his two fingers still buried deeply inside of her. He pushes his tongue into her tight tunnel with his fingers, spreading her wide, before he removes it and then lightly licks around the underside of her hole. With his free hand, he reaches up and spreads her thigh open even wider, exposing her to his wanting mouth, and then he reaches out with his tongue and lightly runs the tip of it over her now exposed, tight little asshole.

Demi knew it was coming, but she still jumps and moans loudly when she feels his tongue caress her most intimate of areas. He doesn't rush her, he just takes his time, gently licking and touching and probing her hole with the tip of his tongue as his fingers still work their magic inside of her.

She is in heaven. Demi tosses her head around from side to side on the bed as she moans, and then she throws her hands up over her head, grabbing at the pillow, the blanket, whatever she can find. She lets her legs drop a little bit further to the sides, relaxing and opening herself up to him completely, allowing Adam to have his way with her.

As he feels her body soften and yield underneath him, Adam begins to grow bolder, consumed with a desire to please her, to make her cum, hard, again and again tonight. Her asshole starts to open more, accepting his intrusion, and so he stiffens his tongue and really starts to fuck her deeply with it, keeping time with the two fingers he can feel still buried deep in her tight pussy, rubbing against his tongue through her thin walls.

Demi cries out loudly, gripping the sheets around her so hard they're pulling off the mattress, desperate for more. She loves the feeling of his warm mouth, his wet tongue, taking her most naughtiest and intimate of holes. At the same time, she can feel his large fingers pushing their way in and out of her other hole, her juices causing a wet, sloppy sound every time he slams into her, rubbing her g spot and pressing against her walls, pushing back into his tongue.

Adam knows a powerful orgasm is going to rip through her soon, but he hasn't quite finished having fun with her yet. As his fingers slide out the next time, he moves his mouth away from her puckered hole and lightly rubs the tip of one of his fingers across it, feeling her jump once more. Then, in one smooth motion, as his finger was nicely lubed from her wet hole, and her ass was primed from his tongue, he gently slides one finger all the way inside her tightest hole, right in to his knuckle.

He holds his hand steady as she moans loudly, throwing her body even further back on the bed as her hips rise up to meet him, allowing her to adjust. Then ever so gently he slides his finger out, almost to the tip, before sliding it back into her again, this time a little bit harder. Her cries grow louder, and he keeps growing bolder, pushing his finger harder and harder into her, exploring her. Then as he slides out for the fourth or fifth time, he switches fingers, sliding his third finger into her ass so he can slide his first two fingers back into her tight pussy.

Demi's moans and cries turn into one long noise of pleasure as she turns her head to the side, burying it in the pillow beside her. Adam smiles a little to himself, loving her reaction to the way he touches her and pleases her, before he lowers his head to her vagina once more, the smell of her much stronger now as wetness leaks out down his fingers and hand. He uses the tip of his tongue to flick at her clit a few times, feeling her tighten around his fingers, before pulling it into his mouth once more, licking on it and sucking it gently.

This is all too much for Demi, and she knows she's going to cum soon, and hard. She can feel one of his fingers sliding in and out of her ass, the pressure intense but not painful now that she's starting to relax and open up, but the naughtiness of it is turning her on like crazy. Then she can feel his other two fingers buried in her other hole at the same time, wiggling, stretching her open, pressing on the thin walls between her pussy and her ass, rubbing against his other finger. But his warm lips and tongue sucking on her clit is the icing on the cake for her, pushing her over the edge.

Demi can feel her orgasm building; her insides start tingling, clenching up, her whole lower body growing tight and tense. Both of her holes begin to squeeze on his fingers, holding them inside of her as her orgasm overtakes her. She throws her legs over his shoulders, pinning his face to her, grabbing at the back of his head and holding him close.

Adam sucks hard on her clit, driving her crazy, wanting to give her the best orgasm she's had in a while. He continues to pound his fingers inside of her, wiggling them, finger fucking both of her holes while she screams in pleasure, her body shaking and spasming on the bed underneath him.

Her walls tighten around him, clenching and unclenching on his fingers like a vice, and cum starts to leak out of her, soaking his fingers and his hand. Adam is dying to lick it all up, but instead he keeps going, sucking and licking harder on her throbbing little clit while he slams his fingers harder and harder inside of her, wiggling deep in her ass and her pussy.

Demi's heart is pounding and she can barely breath, her whole body still shaking and vibrating. Her pussy is still spasming around his fingers, and as she tries to catch her breath she realizes he isn't stopping, and that he has no plans on letting her come down from her high, either.

Her clit is super sensitive now and she tries to wiggle away from him but he holds her close, licking and sucking on it still, making her cry out. He keeps pushing his fingers in and out of her, wetness pooling underneath them now, her asshole more than relaxed and accepting of his exploring finger.

Demi gives up, throwing her head back against the bed once more and giving into the sensations he was giving her, allowing him to tease her, touch her, taste her, and bring her to a second orgasm right after her first.

She arches her back, opening her legs wider, panting now. He lets her clit drop from his lips, flicking it with the tip of his tongue a few times, driving her wild. "Are you going to cum for me again baby?" he asks her, using his free hand to reach up and spread her lips wide, exposing her while his other hand still took her freely, his fingers working magic inside of her.

All Demi can do is moan and thrash around on the bed, so lost to the experience, letting her body go, giving in to the second orgasm that's coursing through her. Adam feels her whole body shudder and tighten around him once more, and then wetness explodes everywhere as she cums even harder this time, feeling more open and relaxed this time than the first. He can feel her walls tighten around his fingers, and he slams them into her a few more times, hitting her g spot roughly, before moving his mouth down to her tight hole to lick her clean.

He slowly removes his hands, and then grabs her by the back of her thighs and pushes her legs up over her hips, completely opening her up to him. Adam leans down and licks her from her asshole to her clit, over and over again, tasting and licking up ever drop while she moans and thrashes below him, overly sensitive now and still trying to come down from that second orgasm that ripped through her.

"Adam," she says, half gasping and half giggling, still shifting around underneath him. "That was intense. I need a minute." Her clit feels like it's on fire, swollen and sensitive, and every time his tongue glides over it her whole body jumps, her toes curling, her hands balled into fists. She can still barely breath, gasping, her chest heaving up and down between her spread open knees.

He finally pulls away from her, although a little reluctantly, but then stays kneeling between her legs for a moment longer, staring at her spread open pussy, both holes wet and wide open on display for him. Although she's exhausted from that intense double orgasm, she feels her insides clench and her pussy twitch in response to being looked at like that, the way he stares at her pussy like he's never seen anything quite as incredible in his entire life.

She gives her body a little wiggle, giving in to being put on display like this. "Are you going to fuck me or what baby?" she asks him, reaching down between her legs and spreading her pussy even wider with both hands, looking him in the eye and biting on her lower lip.

Adam's cock is throbbing in his pants, the inside of his boxers wet with pre-cum. He'd practically been grinding his hips into the bed while he'd ate her out, so desperate to pound himself into her. He doesn't need any more of an invitation from her than that, considering he couldn't be more eager right now. He gets up off the bed for a moment, strips his jeans off in a hurry and then climbs back on between her legs, but stops before he takes her like she's desperately waiting for.

Demi eyes up his dripping cock, her own hands having made their way from holding her pussy open to rubbing her clit, fingers all over her folds, still horny as hell and ready for him. He grabs his cock, stroking it, watching her, and she starts to wonder what's taking him so long when he says to her, "Get up on your knees, I want to take you from behind."

She drops her hands away from herself and slowly rolls over, her legs needing a moment before they can hold her, still feeling slightly shaky from her crazy orgasm. Demi gets to her knees, turned with her back towards him, facing the headboard. She hikes her dress up once more, exposing her round ass to him, and then she bends over slowly, lowering herself to the bed. Now she's face down on the mattress, ass up in the air towards him, hands to her sides, weight on her arms.

Adam watches as she gives her hips a shake once more, everything open and on display for him. This is killing him, and as he watches her wet lips press together and then slide open again, and her little puckered rosebud winks at him, he can take this no longer. He strokes his hard cock once more, grabbing it by the base and running his fist up the length of it, rubbing his thumb over the head to spread some pre-cum around. Then he leans forward and lightly touches the head of it against her opening.

Demi lets out a loud moan, and the moment she tries to thrust her hips backwards, Adam times it well and lets his cock go, pushing forward, slamming his hips into her ass and filling her completely. She cries out, pushing her face into the mattress to muffle it, but Adam reaches down and grabs a handful of her head, pulling her head back, and she gets that much louder now, knowing exactly what he wants to hear.

Adam starts to slam his cock into her, over and over, feeling her silky walls clench and squeeze him as he slides almost all the way out, her lips almost sucking on the head of his cock. With one hand on her hips, he holds her steady and fucks her over and over, his other hand tightly clenching her hair still, forcing her to arch backwards and up towards him.

"Yes, please, fuck me Adam, take me," she pants, arms shaking as she holds herself upwards on the bed. Adam leans down, never breaking stride, pressing his back up against hers as he nibbles and licks on her earlobe, and her whole body trembles in his arms. "Are you going to cum again Demi?" He whispers in her ear, and she simply moans in reply.

He keeps holding her tightly while he fucks her for a few more minutes before he releases her hair, letting her fall back down to the bed. He knows he won't be far behind her with an orgasm of his own, and he wants to go out with a big one.

Adam grabs her around the hips, holding her closer to the inside and stretching his palms out so that his thumbs are closer into her ass cheeks. Then he spreads them, spreading her wide as he does, looking down and watching his cock disappear between her wet pussy lips while her asshole winks at him.

    Demi moans as she buries her face into the mattress in front of her, both embarrassed and turned on at being exposed for him like that. Adam slows his strokes, taking his time and letting his penis ever so gently slide all the way inside of her tight tunnel, feeling her clench and squeeze around him, before he slowly slides all the way out again, watching her lips pull out and pop close as he withdraws.

    Now it's his turn to moan loudly, loving the view in front of him, listening to her moan and pant and beg, feeling his balls begin to tighten as his own orgasm draws near. He digs his thumbs into her ass cheeks again, opening her up once more, and then he leans down and spits on her, watching her jump and squeal as her asshole opens and clenches, letting his spit slide inside.

    Without breaking his slow, teasing stride he reaches over with one hand and rubs his fingers gently along her exposed asshole, and then pushes one inside of her at the same time as his cock fills her pussy.

    "Oh, my god!" She yells loudly, getting up on her elbows so that she has a bit more leverage, beginning to press herself back into him as he slowly fucks her and fingers her asshole at the same time. He grips her ass tightly, holding her open wider as he starts to fuck her harder, and then he lets go and slaps her ass cheek hard, the sound echoing in the hotel room.

    He picks up speed, fucking both of her holes harder now, and they're both moaning, neither of them far from an orgasm. "Fuck, Demi, your ass is so tight," he says to her, sliding his finger in as deep as he can and twisting it around, slamming his cock into her, taking her roughly. She can't even speak anymore, she just moans incoherently as she rolls around on the mattress, ass in the air, hips slamming back into his.

    She lets out a yell, and at the same time he feels her start to spasm and tighten around his finger and his cock, her asshole clenching around him, her pussy feeling like it's milking him. Her body starts to shake against him, and as she moans his name he feels his own cock explode inside of her, his balls tightening and then letting go.

Adam holds her tightly around the hips, his own body shaking as he keeps her steady, his cock twitching deep inside of her, filling her with hot cum. Her slim body still withers around on the bed in front of him, her pussy holding onto him like a vice, her face buried in the mattress and pillow in front of her, but he can hear her gasping for breath.

After a few more strokes he pulls out, letting out a sigh at how sensitive his cock has become as it slides out from her wet tight tunnel. Then he removes his finger from her still spasming asshole and gives her ass another gentle smack before he collapses down on the bed beside her to catch his breath. Her hips give out and she crashes down beside him, snuggling up close and giggling, still feeling high from her orgasm.

Adam wraps his arms around her, pulling her close and kissing her on the top of her forehead, feeling happy and content, and almost ready to fall asleep. That is, until her partially naked, half dress torn body turns towards him and whispers, "Time for a drink and some fresh air before round two?"

Chapter Seventeen

Adam awakens far too early the next morning, his head feeling foggy and pounding with a brutal headache, and a quick glance at the bedside clock shows him that it's barely past 6am. Definitely too soon to be awake after the wild night they'd had the night before. He can't tell if the screaming from inside of his skull is from having too much to drink last night, or from everything that's running through his mind, all the things that he's been putting off that are finally coming back to haunt him this morning, playing back and forth on repeat from the moment he opened his eyes, driving him mad. He'd even been plagued by terrible dreams, and had a very restless sleep.

He looks over beside him to find Demi snuggled up peacefully, still sound asleep and cuddling one of the hotel pillows into her chest, blankets strewed all about them. By how late they stayed up the night before, he doubts she'll be waking up anytime soon, but he is far too restless and his head hurts too much to simply lay here and watch her sleep, knowing that's only going to frustrate him. So instead, he gets up.

Tiptoeing silently though their hotel room, he puts coffee on and uses the washroom, and then he makes himself a big mug of coffee and takes it out onto the balcony to watch the sunrise come up over the ocean, not wanting to wake her until she's ready.

It's a chillier morning than most have been recently, but it's still not too cold for him to sit there in quiet reflection, his mug warming his hands. He finds himself thinking about the night before, about how wonderful everything had felt between them, how right, when they were finally focusing on them and not the things that had been centered about their life so far; crime, robberies, money, dishonesty, and being on the constant go.

Then he finds himself thinking about the plan he's working on with Brandon, and the *why* behind it, even though it revolves around him sneaking around behind

Demi's back and keeping things from her, and also involves pretty much all of those things they wanted to get away from. He's doing this so that they can always live like last night, forever, carefree and happy and able to do whatever they want with their lives, in love and in the moment.

It's right then and there that Adam realizes he would do absolutely anything to make this all work and come together as smoothly as possible. He would sacrifice anything to make her happy, to make her smile, to make her stay with him, and give her the life that he feels she deserves, the life that they both deserve to have together.

The only reason that Adam had even said yes to this robbery in the first place was because it was such a huge pay off with such little work, and because of all Brandon's ins and connections, it was going to be a simple job. Never mind the fact that Brandon was good at what he does, and already had this in the bag. Adam vows to himself that this is going to be the very last crime that they will ever commit.

After this, they will stash the money away somewhere safe, maybe even invest it properly, even though Adam has to admit he knows absolutely nothing about that or how it works, he's sure that Demi does, or that they can learn together. They will buy a beautiful house together here somewhere along the coast, just like she said she wanted, and they will settle down and start a life here together.

Adam thinks about waking up beside her every single morning, snuggling her close, watching the sun rise up over the ocean, having incredible mind blowing sex together every day, in their own beds, all over their own house, never living on the run or on the go again. They'd get married and grow old together, traveling to fancy places, raising their kids, and watching the sunset every night.

He isn't sure where that sudden flood of romantic imagery had come from, but he doesn't mind thinking it over this morning, the thoughts making him happy. Adam smiles to himself, taking a sip of his coffee, his mood now changed from when he'd woken up, the grumpiness subsided, and his head pounding less now, his headache almost forgotten entirely.

Hearing something that draws him out of his thoughts, he looks up to see Demi standing there in the doorway, a sleepy look on her face, pulling the housecoat closer around her against the chill of the morning ocean air. She has a mug of coffee in her own hand, and as she wanders out and takes a seat beside him, she asks him what he was thinking about that had him smiling so hugely this early in the morning.

Adam finds himself flushing, almost as if she's caught him up to something wrong. "Honestly, I was just thinking about how amazing it is that I've got you, and this incredible life we have together," he says to her with a smile, trying to ignore the racing of his heart he feels hammering inside of his chest.

Demi smiles back at him, reaching over and lightly touching his hand, and then she turns her gaze out over the water, watching the sunrise, taking in the beauty of everything around her as she starts her day. She slowly sips from her mug of coffee, feeling tired but content.

Today is the day, Adam thinks to himself, today absolutely has got to be the day. He cannot put this off any longer. He's going to find the right way to talk to her, and tell her the plan and what he's been up to behind her back, like he was supposed to do last night. That's what he'd told Brandon he was going to do. Hell, he should have just told her all of this from the beginning, he finds himself thinking again.

He feels this strong urge inside of him that he's got to do this, now, the sooner the better, before things get out of hand on him. He can't wait until this is a memory like everything else that they've been through, and then they can put this behind them and really move on and start a new life together like she wants, like they deserve.

Chapter Eighteen

By lunch time of that same day though, Adam's happy and carefree feelings that he'd had that morning are long gone. He is irritable, snappy, and finding himself unable to concentrate on anything, constantly wondering when the right time is going to be to talk to her, and how he's going to approach it and bring this up.

Demi can sense that something is off with him, and she's tried to bring it up a few times, but he keeps blowing her off, getting tense and snippy with her, telling her that he's just tired and feeling slightly hungover, and probably had too much sun and beer the day before, and not enough sleep last night.

Every time she brings it up, Adam gets more and more frustrated, not wanting to be cornered by her and put on the spot, and not wanting to talk to her about things before he's good and ready, because he really doesn't even know where to start. He doesn't mean to get rude and short with her, but lying to her again and again is eating him up inside, and he's anxious to figure out a way to talk to her on his terms, even though he's feeling more and more rushed as time passes, like this is falling out of his hands and his control. He's desperate to get this out in the open, and be done with it.

Demi isn't quite sure she believes him, but she doesn't have anything else to go on, nor does she have any reason to think he would be lying to her about anything, so she convinces herself that she's simply being paranoid and needs to drop it, even though that feels impossible.

She takes a deep breath and tries to convince herself to relax. What she really needs though is to take a breather, and to get away from Adam and his grumpy mood for a while, and out of this stuffy hotel room. She tells him that she's going down to the pool for a while, but her voice doesn't even cut through whatever's going on inside of his head, and she needs to repeat herself twice before he actually hears her.

Adam doesn't do much more than nod at her once while looking at his phone when she finally does have his attention, and she lets him know that she's taking her book and some sunscreen and plans to be down at the pool for a while to get some sun and some fresh air. She leaves feeling a little frustrated with him, with herself, and with the whole situation, because she doesn't understand what's happening, or why either of them are feeling the way they do, especially after the amazing vacation they've been having so far. She knows deep down that something isn't right here.

The truth is, Brandon has been blowing Adam's phone up all day, demanding answers, wanting to know what the game plan is, and at this point, Adam's nerves are absolutely shot. Brandon started texting him not long after he had first opened his eyes this morning when he had been unable to sleep, and Brandon hadn't given it a rest since, anxious to get a response back from Adam about their next move.

Brandon is already raring to get the ball rolling and get started, and here Adam is practically sitting around twiddling his thumbs, with no idea how he's going to tell Demi what's going on yet, or what he's been up to. He's terrified to even open his mouth anymore, worried that the wrong thing is going to come out, or that he's going to get mad at her over nothing, simply because of the way that he's feeling.

Because Adam hasn't had a chance to do anything yet, he doesn't answer Brandon, but this doesn't put Brandon off like he had hoped. In fact, it only makes him more and more anxious to get an answer, and so he keeps messaging repeatedly, and even calls a couple of times, desperate to get through. Adam is so grateful that he'd left his phone on silent, although he was still sweating buckets all morning, beside himself that Demi might see his phone over his shoulder, or question him about who could possibly be blowing his phone up like that, calling and texting him off the hook, or even why he was glued to it so much today.

He hates the way that he's feeling, guilt washing over him in waves like a disease, constantly feeling miserable, and he's short and snappy all day even though he doesn't mean to be. He feels sick to his stomach, like he's cheating, like he's doing something terribly wrong behind her back, and he's repeatedly mad at himself for chickening out every time he gets a chance to talk to her. He desperately needs to get all of this out in the open, before he really is sick.

Once he hears the hotel door slam shut behind Demi, Adam lets out a long breath he hadn't even realized that he'd been holding. He doesn't feel any less stressed now that she's out of the room, but a little bit of peace and quiet and alone time may be exactly what he needs to talk to Brandon once more, so they could both talk some sense into Adam, and then he could make a god damn plan so that he can get this done and over with.

Adam wanders around the room for a few minutes, phone in hand, trying to type out a couple of novel texts to Brandon, desperate to fill him in and let out everything that building up in his head at the same time. His thoughts are spiraling though, scattered and jumping from this to that, and he knows there's far too much he wants and needs to say to Brandon that a couple of texts simply won't cut it. He grabs a beer from the mini fridge and starts to make his way to the balcony doors, thinking he'd sit out there and keep an eye on Demi down by the pool while he catches up with Brandon on the phone.

He's barely made it to the balcony doors when his cell phone lights up in his hands once more. He laughs to himself, thinking about how damn persistent Brandon can be when he really wants something, and then he answers it, juggling the beer in one hand while standing in the doorway and holding his phone to his ear with the other.

Brandon is laughing at him over the phone, but the tone in his voice lets Adam know that part of him doesn't think this is very funny at all. "I can't believe that you still haven't told her about this yet," Brandon says to him with a chuckle, "this is ridiculous man. Who wears the pants in that relationship? You are wasting all of our time here, and we need to be taking this seriously." His tone drops again at the end, from slightly laughing to full on annoyance, and then he keeps going, making sure that Adam knows just how pissed off about this he is. Brandon has a point to make here, he wants Adam to know that he was doing this for them in the first place. He didn't *have* to include Adam and Demi in this scheme, he *wanted* to help them out, but Adam needs to get with the program.

Adam has to cut him off a few times, getting annoyed himself, thinking that Brandon is getting way too worked up, and way too fast. "Brandon!" He practically yells into the phone, interrupting his buddy. "You need to calm down, I'm barely a day behind schedule here, relax. I *am* going to tell Demi about this robbery! Hell, she has a part to play you know. I'm not just, *not* going to tell her. I just need to make sure it's the right time. You don't know what our relationship is like, or how fragile she can be. Just give me a little bit more time, alright? I'm not trying to dick you around. This robbery is going to happen."

Brandon agrees to give him a little more time like he's asked, although he does so reluctantly, and then the guys end their phone call with Adam promising to touch base with him again later that evening. Adam hits the end call button and then shuts his phone off altogether, feeling more frustrated now than before he'd even spoke to Brandon again. He feels like things are happening way too fast, and he hasn't even had a real chance to get a handle on everything yet.

Still standing in the half open door way, he turns around, thinking he might just get changed and grab a towel and head down to the pool with Demi instead, needing to blow off some steam now himself. But then he looks up to see her standing there in the middle of the hotel room, her jaw wide open and a look of total heart break and disbelief all over her face. She has her towel and book in one hand, but now she holds a bottle of juice in her other, what she'd forgotten and came back to grab from the mini fridge after buying it the evening before.

As far as Demi is concerned, it feels like Adam just slapped her across the face. Here she is, thinking that he's grumpy with her for some stupid reason she can't think of yet, or maybe he really did just sleep awful and woke up hung over and snappy with her, but no. He's miserable because he's been sneaking around behind her back, talking to Brandon of all people, her original kidnapper, someone Adam had sworn up and down that he didn't have any contact with anymore.

And yet, here he was, planning some sort of robbery with the guy, and planning to involve her in it too, without even talking to her about it! When they were supposed to be here on vacation, relaxing and letting that whole part of their life and their relationship go, leaving it in the past where it belongs. Her stomach turns, and she feels like she may throw up. He's been telling her nothing but lies, and she doesn't even know how far back they go.

The look on her face is as clear as day to Adam. Heartbreak, betrayal, hurt, it's enough to stop Adam's breath in his throat and his heart in his chest. At the same time that he watches a tear slide down her cheek, he feels his cell phone slip from his hand and hit the floor, echoing extra loudly in the silence of their hotel room.

Chapter Nineteen

"What in the ever loving fuck is going on?" Demi hears herself say, but it comes out in a hoarse whisper that doesn't even sound like her own voice. She doesn't feel like herself right now either, and barely even hears herself talking. She feels like she is outside of her body, floating, watching all of this unfold as if she is someone else, feeling sad and confused, and so very lost.

Adam feels like he's coming apart at the seams. His worst fears have come true, everything is spiraling out of his control, and fast, and he doesn't even know what he's supposed to tell her now, or have a clue where to even begin.

"Demi, fuck I am so sorry, I promise you, I never meant to hide any of this from you, not like this. I should have just told you right away when he first contacted me, I just wanted to make a plan and figure out what was actually going on first before I talked to you about it. I don't know what I was even thinking. I'm so, so sorry baby."

He feels the words fall flat on his lips, and he knows he may as well not have said anything at all, she may as well be deaf for all she actually heard what he had to say. Or for how much she truly cares for what he has to say right now, either.

"You *lied* to me Adam! How could you!" She yells at him, and her voice cracks in the middle, as the flood gate of tears that she's holding back threatens to burst open. "Was this the whole reason that you even agreed to come here with me, and take this "vacation" with me," she says, making quotations in the air with her hands when she says "vacation", clearly now believing he'd only done this because he'd had ulterior motives that had nothing to do with her, or them, at all.

"Did you even ever *want* to be here on vacation with me?" She continues, her voice growing high, and then she keeps on yelling before he can even reply, not caring for an answer, feeling like she already knows it. "Was this ever something you would have done with me at all, if it wasn't for Brandon and his stupid money, his stupid robberies and crimes? Is this why you've been so grumpy and distant with me lately, because you didn't want to be here with me at all? You'd rather be planning a fucking robbery with your buddy?"

Demi can tell that she's borderline hysterical right now, and Adam keeps trying to cut her off and say something, but she isn't done yet. She has more pouring through her veins, she's hurt and confused and angry, and Adam is damn well going to know how badly he's broken her heart. He's going to hear everything that she has to say before she's done.

"Every single time that you told me that everything was fine, that you were just tired, or that you didn't sleep well, or that you were hung over, or sick of driving, I *knew* deep down in my soul that you were fucking LYING to me, over and over and over again. How could you do that to me Adam? How am I supposed to trust you when all you do is lie? All of this has been a damn lie."

Her voice cracks once more at the end there, and when it does, this time, she may as well have slapped him. He feels all the wind get knocked out of him at the sound of her voice, and it's hard to breathe. It's in that moment that he realizes how stupid he's been, how fragile their relationship really is, and how strongly she feels about putting all of this behind them. He realizes how different they are from each other right then, and how awful he must look to her, having been doing all of this from his point of view, his wants, his needs, never actually considering what this would do to her and their relationship.

Adam starts trying to reason with her, to explain himself, desperate to calm her down and to get her to see his side of things, and why he'd done what he had. "Demi, no, that's not how I wanted you to take this. And yes, I lied, but I did actually want to be here with you too! One thing has nothing to do with the other, I swear. I just couldn't stop thinking about our money situation, and when the opportunity arose, I took it. I know our stash isn't going to last us forever, and I wanted to be able to give you the whole world, and everything you've ever wanted. I never meant to hurt you."

Now it's Adam's turn for his voice to crack, still standing there by the balcony door, shifting his weight from foot to foot. He's scared to move, scared to get too close to her, but desperately needing to run to her, to hold her, to squeeze her close to him and kiss her deeply, making her feel like he loves her and that everything is going to be ok.

"Adam," she says, her voice sounding flat as his name flows past her lips, her eyes red and swollen and dark, brimming with tears. "How can you be so fucking stupid? YOU are all I ever wanted. Our life together, our love, our TRUST we were building, our future, that's what I wanted, that's my whole world, and none of that depends on fucking MONEY! Don't you get it? It depends on us trusting each other, building together, and I cannot even trust a word that comes out of your mouth right now. Who knows how long you've been lying to me for?!"

Demi breaks down totally now, yelling at him, sobbing, letting the tears flow freely. She throws herself down on the couch, her legs feeling shaky and numb, unable to support her any longer.

Adam wants to comfort her. Desperately. He doesn't know how, but he knows he needs to make this right; that this is all his fault. But when he steps towards her, when he tries to get close to where she's strewn herself, sobbing on the couch, she screams at him, yelling for him to get away and to give her some space, that she can't even think straight, and certainly doesn't want him in her face right now.

Not knowing what else to do, he freezes in place, shifting once more nervously from foot to foot, feeling his heart pounding so hard it feels like it may burst right out of his chest. His stomach is in a knot, and his palms are soaked in sweat, balled into fists, and his knees are shaky.

He would give anything to be able to go back in time and fix this, and make it right. He doesn't even know where to go from here.

Demi takes a deep breath between sobs, trying to contain herself while her whole body is vibrating. From hurt, or anger, she isn't entirely sure which. It could be both right now. "I don't even know if anything you've ever said to me is true." She says to him, her voice sounding firmer now, more angry, less tearful. "You've told me numerous time that you don't talk to him anymore, but you sure sounded buddy buddy on the fucking phone, like that wasn't the first conversation you've had with him since the night we left town. You looked me right in the eyes and LIED to me!! How could you do this to me? How LONG have you been lying to me for? Our entire relationship? I can't believe you did this!"

She throws her arms up into the air in exasperation when she says this, damn near yelling once more, and then drops them into her lap feeling defeated and exhausted. Then she starts to sob once more, and drops her head into her hands as well, letting the tears flow even harder now that she's said all she can in the moment.

But now Adam finds himself getting frustrated and mad at the situation as well, and he hasn't nearly said all he has to say yet, especially since she'd kept cutting him off. "I was your kidnapper too remember!" He yells at her, and Demi's head jerks up, eyes wide, not expecting to hear that, or that tone come from him. They'd never fought much, and when they had, he had not often fought back against her.

"Brandon's not the only one that snuck in your room that night, kidnapped you while you were sleeping, and held you hostage for almost a week, I was there too! But you fell in love with me, and clearly, have no problem being with me! That says something, about the both of us. And Brandon isn't a bad person either, nor is he even the one who's at fault in any of this. I am. He's just trying to help us out, because this is a LOT of money that's at stake here, that could truly set us up for the rest of our lives.

This is MY fault, Demi, and I know I fucked up here, big time. I'm so sorry. But I had my reasons. Please. Let me make this up to you somehow."

With all of that being said, and now feeling at a loss, Adam reaches into his pocket with a shaky hand and pulls the engagement ring out, watching Demi's eyes widen as he does so, wishing he knew what that look meant, and wishing with everything in his soul that he was doing this under any other circumstances.

"I love you Demi, I love you with everything that I have. I want to marry you, and I want to spend my life with you. I want you to be my wife. I was doing all of this for YOU, for us, for our future. You're all that I wanted, even if I've been an idiot about showing you."

He takes a deep breath and then takes two steps forward, getting closer to where she's sitting on the couch still, and he drops himself down onto one knee. "This isn't how I saw myself doing this a thousand times over in my head, not one single time did this scenario pop in there, but I'm doing it this way anyway, fuck, even if that's a terrible joke. Demi Ramora, will you marry me?"

She doesn't say anything for a moment, she just looks at him. And the look on her face, her sunken, red, hollow eyes, brimming with tears, and the lack of the smile that should be there, that smile that lights up his whole world, tells him everything he needs to know, without her making a sound. She may as well have sucker punched him in the gut, all the wind gets knocked out of him again in one moment.

"You simply don't get it Adam, do you?" She says, and her voice is just as hollow as her eyes, flat and void of all the happiness and love that usually fills them. "You lied to me. Over and over again, you looked me in the eyes and YOU LIED TO ME! Everything I have ever wanted, all I ever needed in life, was you. It was us. Together. What we were building. It was THIS!" When she says this last bit, she swings her arms around, pointing at the messy hotel room, evidence of a wild life on the run.

"Whatever the future had planned for us, all that

ever mattered to me was here in the moment with you. What we were building together, our life, meant more to me than all the riches in the world. I gave UP all of that for YOU in the first place. I can't even think about building a life with you anymore, when I can't even trust you. When you don't even trust ME enough to open up and talk to me and involve me in your life."

Demi can feel herself growing calm in the midst of her hysteria, and the sadness that she was feeling is slowly growing into anger, a calm, cut like a knife anger. She needs to get out of here, now.

"Adam, what you've done is inexcusable. You went behind my back and started planning this huge, life changing thing, that involved me, without even talking to me about it, WHILE YOU WERE PLANNING TO PROPOSE TO ME. And you were doing all of this with Brandon! And to top it off, this was shit you knew I wanted to put behind us. I seriously can't even think straight right now, I am SO mad at you, and so beside myself with all of this. What you've done doesn't show me you love me. This isn't what you do to someone you love. All we had between us was us, was our love and our trust. I feel like you've shattered everything we had, including my fucking heart."

Demi jumps up as she finishes her sentence, feeling sick to her stomach, tears falling so fast that she can barely see, her whole body feeling tingly and numb. She can't breathe, and all she can think about now is getting out of here, getting away from him, getting out of this room and into the fresh air, and putting as much distance between her and this as she can right now.

Adam gets up from his knees, feeling lost and bewildered at everything that's happening and at how fast it all seems to be unraveling too. He's mad at himself and at Demi for the way she's over reacting, and he's feeling lost and confused at what to do next, and how to stop everything from spiraling through his fingers.

He doesn't even know what to say to make her stay, but he begs her to anyways, trying to grab at her arm, but she shrugs him off, demanding that he let her go. "What do you mean, go? Where?" He says, her words stopping him in his tracks, leaving him standing there in disbelief, watching her as she starts to throw a couple of her things into her overnight bag. It hits him just then how serious she really is about this.

      Demi doesn't answer him, she doesn't say another word at all. She just lets the tears fall and sniffles a few times as she grabs whatever she can think of that's important to have right now, including her purse, passport and some money, and then she leaves, walking out the door and slamming it behind her as Adam still stands there, pleading with her to stay.

Chapter Twenty

As Adam watches the door slam shut behind her, he hears an awful sound fill the room, and as he drops back down to his knees on the floor, he realizes the sound is coming from him. He's the one making that terribly, gut wrenching noise from the back of his throat as a hundred different emotions overwhelm him all at once, threatening to explode.

He doesn't even understand how everything just happened so fast, or how it all spiraled out of his control before he really had a good chance to explain anything, or really talk to her and get through to her.

Maybe he hadn't seen things from her point of view, hadn't really seen this as betraying her or doing something that was so dishonest it was worth destroying their relationship over, because he had always planned to talk to her about this and open up to her and include in it her long before it happened. He had just been trying to figure out the right time and the right way to bring it all up to her.

He can see now from her side of things how wrong he'd been. He should have included her from the get go, and never lied to her at all. Their relationship is fragile, and clearly built on a shaky ground of trust, trust he had destroyed the moment he had gone behind her back like that. She had a point, how could he expect her to start a life with him, when he hadn't given her a solid ground to build that life on.

However, he's filled with a lot of anger at her too, because he feels like she over reacted before he'd truly had a chance to explain himself. This wasn't like she'd come back to the hotel and caught him in bed with another woman. He was doing this for them, because he loves her so much and wants to make everything perfect for her, so they can spend the rest of their lives together the way she wants and deserves.

Adam can't let her walk out of the hotel like this. He

has so much he still needs to say to her, this isn't how things are supposed to end, and he simply won't let it.

He takes a deep breath, feeling his whole body vibrating with a hundred different emotions, and then he wipes his cheeks dry and forces himself to his feet. He grabs his hotel keys and nothing else, not even bothering to put shoes on, and then he chases out after her, out in the hallway in his bare feet and running down towards the elevators that she'd already gone down.

Demi is feeling so lost, and confused, her head pounding, she can't even think straight, or think about where she's really going, or what she's going to do next. Leaving had been on such a whim, she's still in her bathing suit with a shall wrapped around her, but she'd thrown some clothes into her overnight bag, and plans to change once she's had some time to get her head together.

But at that moment in the hotel room, she had wanted nothing more than to get away from him, to put as much distance between them as possible. She had never even given much thought to all of the material objects she was leaving behind; her whole life was with him, there in that hotel room. She had just needed so very badly to get away from this whole situation that he'd created that she was willing to leave it all behind her.

This was the second time that he had gone behind her back about something like this. He had given her reason to mistrust him more than once now, and this time, this one was a big one. It hit her hard. It touched on a nerve inside of her that the other time hadn't, because this time, it had involved Brandon, and that was too close to home.

Suddenly, it had felt like she was back at the farm house all over again, kidnapped, just along for the ride without a say about what was going on in her life. She was in the dark again while these two guys made plans for them and dragged her along, not telling her anything. And Adam had been planning to ask her to marry him at the same damn time, while doing all of this behind her back.

The thought makes her feel absolutely sick to her

stomach. She's so confused, and feels so destroyed. It feels like he's tainted everything they had. This was the man she loved, the man she had given up everything for. What had he done, and what was she supposed to do now?

 The elevator pings and opens at the lobby, and Demi doesn't even think twice as she grabs her bag by the handle and walks out. She wanders straight through the lobby, not really seeing anything around her, too lost in thought, trying to keep the tears at bay until she has a chance to be alone, and really absorb what's happening.

 Demi throws open the main hotel doors and wanders out into the sunshine, and the sudden overload of noise, heat and brightness overwhelms her as she's feeling so miserable and caught up in her head. She hails the first cab she sees there waiting, and then, with no other options in mind that she can think of, she tells the driver to take her to the airport. She never even turns around, never glancing behind her to give a second thought for Adam, whose now barreling out of the elevators inside of the hotel. She simply puts herself on auto pilot, and tries not to think about what's actually happening right now.

 Adam's practically running, breathing heavy, gasping, eyes wide, bare feet slapping and echoing on the the tiled floor. He doesn't care how big of a scene he's making, or what kind of a sight he must look like to the random people he passes, all he cares about is finding Demi.

 People are staring at him while he races around the lobby, trying to find her, looking in the restaurant, and then out into the parking lot, feeling more and more frustrated with every passing moment that he can't find her.

 He forces himself to calm down and he gets back on the elevator, hitting the button frantically, ignoring the people still staring at him, and he makes his way back up to their room when he can't find her. Opening the door to their room now that he's been gone for a few minutes, he's hit with the scent of her, and her perfume, and seeing her left behind clothes scattered all over the floor cuts him to the bone.

He crosses the room and quickly snatches his phone up off the floor where it dropped earlier. He turns it on, impatiently pacing around while he does, unable to sit still, needing to find her. He's dialing her number before it's even finished loading in his hand, but when it goes straight to her voicemail, meaning her phone is off, he cries out loud, unable to hold in his anger anymore.

Adam has to resist the urge to throw his phone across the room into the wall and watch it break into a thousand pieces. Instead he finds himself collapsing once more, this time falling into the bed they had shared only a few short hours ago. He pulls the blankets close to him, cuddling them into his chest, inhaling her scent, and he feels his own eyes well up with tears once more.

What the hell had just happened, he thought to himself again, letting out a moan of frustration and clinging the blankets close, terrified that he may be losing her. How could he have been such a fool, so blinded by money, that he'd let her slip away?

Chapter Twenty-One

With a heavy, heavy heart, and with what seems like more baggage under her eyes than with her for carry on, Demi waits nervously and anxiously in line for her flight. She still doesn't quite feel like herself; from the moment she'd walked back into their hotel room and realized that not only had he not heard her come back in, still so preoccupied on the phone, but that he'd also been on the phone with Brandon, she'd felt like she'd been floating, having some sort of out of body experience.

She remembers feeling trapped and panicked and being so very fucking mad at him, and then she remembers grabbing a handful of her things in a haste, mostly just the important things, throwing them into her bag and then storming out of the room and grabbing the next elevator down to the lobby.

She also remembers hailing a cab, and getting into it, telling the driver to bring her to the airport, but all of that feels like she was watching it happen to someone else, like a movie, not things that she herself had done only hours before.

When she'd arrived at the airport, she'd even remembered to find a washroom and get herself changed, as she was still wearing the bathing suit that she'd put on with plans to go to the pool for a few hours to get away from Adam's grumpy mood. That seems like a whole other lifetime ago, and now here she is, getting ready to leave much farther away from him than the hotel pool.

Uncertainty, anger and sadness run through her head, plus thoughts and images of their life together all blend in with images of him on the phone, hearing his plans echoing over and over again in her mind. Then she sees him getting down on one knee again, proposing to her while her heart is breaking. All of this is driving her crazy.

She keeps glancing down at her phone every few minutes even though she knows he can't reach her. She's blocked his number and any incoming calls hours ago. He has no idea where to find her, where she is, how to reach her, and for the moment, she's fine with that.

Demi doesn't know what she's doing anyways. She isn't thinking clearly, and has no idea if she's even making the right decisions right now, thinking while so emotional, so caught up in what's happening, but she isn't willing to dig deep enough into what's going on to figure it out, either.

She'd been pacing the airport well into the evening hours, waiting for her red-eye flight. On a whim, to pass the time, she'd even bought a pair of scissors and taken them to the bathroom and hacked a chunk of her hair off, and now it sat slightly curly and barely brushing the back of her shoulders. She wasn't sure what she was doing right now, but she was ready for a start fresh. Her flight was here, waiting for her to board, and she wasn't going to let herself think twice about it. She was leaving.

It was impossible for her to think clearly around Adam, she knew that. She was drawn to him like a magnet, and was always willing to forgive him for his issues even when she didn't want to, because she always found herself giving in. She was not going to heal from something that had hurt her as bad as this had in the same environment that had hurt her in the first place. If things were meant to be between them, then they would work themselves out over time.

But this life that they'd been living, always traveling, committing crimes and living on the run, running from reality more than anything, living like a modern day Bonnie and Clyde, that wasn't healthy, that wasn't a real relationship, and not something that she wanted to spend the rest of her life doing either. It was all sexual chemistry and teenage dreams.

And then there was this feeling in her bones right now, this experience of having had the only man she'd truly opened up to enough to love, ripping her heart out and betraying her like this; she wasn't herself right now and she knew that. She needed to get away from all of this, far away, and get back to herself. She needed to heal.

She would call Adam when she got settled, back to her hometown and her old house, and she figured out what it was that she needed to say. Maybe they would be able to fix things, but then again, she thought with a heavy sigh, sniffling a sob in the crowded airport, people all around her but feeling so alone, maybe they wouldn't be able to fix things at all.

Slowly, she handed over her pass and boarded the plane. As she walked down the walkway, she found herself thinking, at what point do you realize the difference between love, and a life lesson, and is there really a difference at all? She shook her head, not knowing where that thought had even come from. She needed some space. A few days, a week, she didn't know for sure.

What she did know was that she needed to find herself again. The real Demi. Who she was before he'd kidnapped her in the dead of the night, and turned her whole life upside down for love. Or, who she was now, after all of this had shaped her and changed her into someone new.

The End.... For Now.

Please follow me on social media, Author Carissa McIntyre, Lady Mack, for updates on all my newest work!

www.ladymackpublishing.com

All my love,
Lady Mack,
Author Carissa McIntyre xoxo

Made in the USA
Columbia, SC
20 November 2020